THE FOUR HORSEMEN: LEGACY

A REVERSE HAREM SERIES

LJ SWALLOW

Editing by Hot Tree Editing

Cover Designed by TakeCover Designs

The Four Horsemen: Legacy
A Reverse Harem Series

What's worse than being pursued by the Four Horsemen? Discovering you're the Fifth.

Verity Jameson's day switches from mundane to disastrous when she runs down a stranger with her car. Fortunately for Vee, she can't kill Death.

Death, who just happens to be one of the Four Horsemen, and he's looking for her.

The Four Horsemen spend life preventing the end of the world, not bringing on an apocalypse. As gatekeepers of the portals which exist between the human world and other realms, the team fight to keep the portals closed and the supernatural forces under control. Without their fifth member, the Four Horsemen are losing the battle.

Now they've found Verity and what they tell her goes far beyond the conspiracy theories Vee spends her free time investigating.

A new life with four dark, sexy and dangerous men fighting demons, vampires and fae? Not what Vee had planned, but a hell of a lot more interesting than her boring job in tech support. So what happens when the unbreakable bond of the Five takes control in a way none of them expected?

1

VERITY

Oh crap, I told the truth again.

Victoria's hand freezes in the air, midway through applying bright pink lipstick, and her stunned expression reflects in the mirror. I stand behind and cringe at her reaction to my words.

"I mean, your hair's already a lovely colour, and your new highlights look—" *Stop, Verity.* "I didn't mean your hair looks bad, just unusual." I fight chewing on my knuckles to stop myself spouting any more unwelcome truth to my work colleague.

I hate lying.

Absolutely cannot deal with people who lie. Like, lose my shit cannot deal with. My inability to tell a lie myself, even the tiny white variety, kills me too. Why couldn't my parents choose a different virtue to name me after? Hope,

Faith, Grace? I'd take anything but the name meaning truth, because I'm sure this cursed me to lose friends due to my blunt truthful nature. Took me years to realise when girls say "be honest" that this is code for "don't tell somebody their ass does in fact look big in that." I glance at Victoria's sour face beneath her unfortunate hair.

Why do girls ask me these questions? Can't they see my lacking interest in all this? My long brown hair sees a pair of scissor once a year; I've never coloured it and styling equals brushing the thick mane into a ponytail. I'm a jeans and T-shirt girl and avoid high heels at all costs because they draw attention to my taller than average, slim figure. Make-up? I have no clue what suits me so I stick to occasional lip gloss and mascara.

My obsessions lie elsewhere and not with my appearance.

“Well, I like the colour," Victoria replies in a cool voice as she inspects her lipstick.

I calculate how many seconds it would take to vacate the bathrooms as the uncomfortable heat builds inside.

Her friend, Charlotte, exits a stall behind me and shakes her blue silk shirtsleeves away from her wrists before flicking on the tap. “What's wrong, babe?” asks Charlotte as she rinses her hands and shakes water from her fingertips as if it's poison.

“Verity doesn't like my new hair colour.” She throws me a disdainful look.

The telecommunications company I work for doesn't have a uniform, but some girls manage to turn the day into a daily fashion competition. I often admire them, but for their commitment to perfection and not their work status. No, I admire anybody who climbs out of bed an hour earlier than necessary to torture themselves with straightening tongs. From the back, I can't tell Charlotte and Victoria apart, they're so similar. I believe in a lot of weird crap, clones included, but despite their almost identical appearance, Charlotte and Victoria are only clones of the fashionista variety. If scientists scientifically engineered people, they'd choose higher intelligence—and beauty that doesn't come in tubes from Sephora.

"So, lovely, are you coming to Dana's party tonight?" asks Victoria.

Her pointed comment stabs greater than the rejection.

Another side effect of my inability to lie is I have no social life. Partly my fault for staying in the small town I've spent my twenty-one years in, while friends moved away to bigger and brighter lives. The ones who did stay have kids now, and I'm not keen on spending time around happy families.

Nope, I live with my cat in a flat above a shop, where I head home after work and watch bad TV or work on my blog. Some would call me a "conspiracy theorist." I prefer the term "looking for the truth." The corporations and governments present a world they want everyone to believe exists, hiding the corruption and their interference. Who's really in control? It doesn't matter who we vote for in our democracy, the same background people run the whole show. Illuminati? Yeah, I'm pretty damn sure they exist.

My weird obsession I talk about at any opportunity suggests another reason I'm rarely invited to "'clone wars" or whatever the hell these girls do when they get together.

“I am. Did you invite the new guy to the party?” asks Charlotte.

Victoria rubs her lips together and touches the corner of her mouth. “Seriously? He works with the *geeks* and never speaks to me.”

Another comment thrown in my direction—the girl buried in the support section who avoids talking to others.

But I know who they’re talking about. I don’t know him per se, but his arrival several weeks ago ruffled feathers and set hormones ablaze. There's no possibility this guy could duck under the radar, if not for his height alone. I haven't stood close enough to him to gauge our height difference, but from a distance, I'd say he's well over six feet tall. Shirt and trousers designed for office work don't equal sexy, but they certainly don't hide his solid muscle.

I admit to sneaking a look at his ass one day last week, which I can also give a big thumbs up to. I bit off the plastic end of my pen in surprise when he turned around to look at me, and I spent the rest of the day with blue ink smearing my lips. Amusement sparkled in his eyes as if he were aware I was perving on him, but his heavy browed face held friendliness, rather than an arrogance often accompanying smoking-hot dudes.

"Well, he finally spoke to *me,* and I found out his name is Heath." Charlotte throws Victoria a sly smile. "Unfortunately he was too busy to stop and chat for long."

I smile at the floor in satisfied amusement that he's not interested in her flirting.

"So you didn't invite him to the party?" asks Victoria.

"No. I didn't have a chance." Charlotte wipes her

hands on a paper towel and picks up her purse. "Maybe next time."

"He said that or you're guessing?"

Charlotte glances at me and leans forward to whisper something in her friend's ear. They giggle, the noise grating like nails down a chalkboard. Without another word to me, the girls walk away. The heavy bathroom door clunks closed leaving me and my truthful mouth behind.

2

VERITY

Darkness and pouring rain greet me as I leave work. Not surprising for an English autumn, but as I drive the ferocity blurs my windscreen and the sound drowns out the music playing. The screen mists too, and I crank up the air-con to blast heat at the window. Maybe I should stop until the weather clears a little?

I squint through the misted window, relieved I'm almost home, and take a right turn into the narrow street leading to the parking area behind the building. A dark shape looms in the road before me, and I have milliseconds to register the tall figure's a person before slamming on my brakes. The tyres skid on the wet road as I attempt to switch the car's trajectory. Instead of remaining still, the figure steps in the same direction, and straight in front of the car.

The next noise sickens my stomach and launches me into full-blown panic mode. A bang, and the figure falling from view. I'm stunned for a second, frozen in indecision. *Uh, you hit somebody, and you're sitting in the car still?* With trembling fingers, I dig around in my purse and pull out my phone, opening the car door with my other hand.

Heart pounding at what I might see on the road, I rush around to the front of the car as I fumble to dial emergency services.

A man sits on the tarmac, hand on the side of his head. Noticing me, he jumps to his feet and sways.

"Shit," he mutters.

In the dark, all I can see is he's tall, wearing jeans and a combat style jacket. His hair, longer at the sides, falls into his face as steadies himself on the car.

And that he stands beside an impressive dent.

I blink away the rain falling onto my eyelashes and soaking my hair. "I'm so sorry; I didn't see you. Are you okay?"

"Who are you calling?" He speaks in a low voice with a cultured English accent, with no hint of anger—or pain.

"An ambulance."

"I don't need an ambulance."

"I just hit you with my car, at a speed road safety experts suggest would kill a small child."

"Do I look like a small child?" He moves away from the car and straightens, wiping at his damp jeans and jacket sleeves.

"No, but you dented my car." I gesture at the front.

The guy coughs a laugh. "I apologise for the damage."

"No, no. I mean, look at the dent. Why aren't you hurt?"

"The car didn't hit me that hard. Your bodywork must be shit."

"You made a bang. A loud one."

"I made a bang?" The amusement tinges his voice.

The rain pours over us as if someone's standing above hosing icy water on our heads. My car headlights shine through the downpour, the only light, as we stand in the dark entrance to the car park. Nobody else is around; a couple of cars are in their resident bays, and others pass along the town street a few hundred metres away.

"I think you need checking out by a doctor. You might have a concussion." I hold the now damp phone against my ear and recoil when the guy steps forward.

He curls a hand around mine to pull the phone away. His face is undamaged; mouth pursed, large eyes fixed on mine. My already panicked heart rate picks up again at his touch, how his fingers are warm against my cold ones. Those lips... exactly the kind a girl could tug into her mouth and bite.

I allow him to take my phone, unable to keep up with the situation. The rain continues to pelt down, soaking our clothes.

I know this man.

Well, his ass anyway.

"Are you the new guy from work?" I blurt.

"New guy?" He peers at me. "Oh. You work at Alphanet too. Don't you?"

He recognises me? "Yes."

"I'm Heath. Nice to meet you. Kind of." He nods at me, rain dripping from his long fringe and along his cheek. I lick my lips as I watch the raindrops cross his. "You should go home and lie down for the shock," he says in a soft voice.

"I am home," I stammer and point at the building. "Almost."

I step backwards to shelter beneath the building's overhanging eaves; my work shirt sticks to my body, water running down my legs and into my sneakers.

How is he okay? I just bloody slammed my car into him.

"Are you telling me I'm the one who needs medical help here?" I ask.

"Well, I don't." He dips his head and joins me in my sheltered place.

My panicked mind speeds up with stories about people who pretend to be injured, who abduct people and rob them, or worse. Men who charm themselves into women's homes. What if he knows I live alone? Is planning to...

I flinch away from him. "Right. Thanks. If you really are okay, maybe I should go inside. Could I have my phone, please?"

"Seriously, Verity, I'm not about to hurt you." He drops the phone into my palm.

Whoa. I step sideways and eye my car, planning an escape. "First, Mr. Ironman, how do you know my name when you've never spoken to me? And secondly, how do I know you won't hurt me?"

He crosses his arms. "Firstly, Miss Bad Driver, I work with you. And secondly, you have a keen sense for bullshit. Am I lying?"

He's correct. I'd detect in a heartbeat if he lied. I wipe

water from my face with cold hands and attempt to make out his features. “How would you know...?” I trail off.

“I’ll prove it.” He pulls a lanyard from his pocket. "I've worked at Alphanet for three weeks. I thought you'd seen me around?"

The tug at the corner of his mouth confirms it. He knows who I am, caught me staring at his ass the other day, so why pretend otherwise?

Keeping my eyes on his, I take the lanyard from his hands and study the card. Heath Landon. His employer number. A criminally attractive photo. The “serial killer” look is standard for everybody, on any photo taken for ID, not his. Seriously, you should see my passport. I look like a freaking zombie.

"Then why are you lurking near my house? Are you stalking me?" I demand.

"Near your house? I was crossing the street on my way to the pub, and you mowed into me!"

Again, Heath isn't lying; my strange sixth sense tells me that. Plus, I do live on a street in the centre of town, not far from pubs and shops.

"Right. Sorry," I mumble and hand back the lanyard. "And you're sure you're okay?" The bizarreness of the situation bites. "Really, I feel responsible. Like you might have internal injuries or something. People don't stand and walk away when cars hit them."

"Evidently they do." He drags a phone from his jacket and frowns down at the screen. "You broke my phone though."

"Sorry. I can pay to replace it?" I wrinkle my nose, my wet clothes becoming more uncomfortable as the moments pass. "I need to go inside. Do you want to uh...?

I can get you a coffee or... I can take you to Emergency to get checked out by a doctor?"

Heath chews on his lip and stares behind me, losing all interest in our conversation. I shiver as if somebody standing behind ran fingers along my spine, then dug their fingers into my hair.

I turn my head. A tall figure crosses the car park on the other side of the small space, head bowed against the rain. Heath steps closer to me, and I move away when his hand touches my arm. *Personal space, much?*

Heath continues to watch the male figure until he rounds the corner and into the street, out of view.

Blinking, he rubs a hand across his damp hair. "Listen, I need to go. I'm meeting friends, and I'm late. How about I find you tomorrow when we're at work and prove that I'm okay? Buy me a coffee, then?" He lifts up one arm, coat torn, revealing a chequered shirt beneath. "Maybe compensation for ruining my clothes."

His taciturn face lights as his mouth pulls into a teasing grin, sharpening his cheekbones.

My head spins at the situation. What am I supposed to do? I can't force Heath to stay with me or into my home, or bundle him into my car and drive him to the hospital. I doubt I could physically move a guy that solid anywhere; it's a good thing he isn't still lying on the ground injured. I attempt to find words relevant to the situation, but speech fails me.

"I'll be with my friends. If I collapse with internal bleeding, they can help."

Shit. "Do you think you might?"

"No. I don't. Park your car, go home, and warm up. See you tomorrow."

I open my mouth to protest, but before I can utter a word, Heath hunches his shoulders and walks away through the rain. I watch for a limp, or in case he crumples to the ground. I've heard of male bravado, but this is ridiculous. Yet the whole time I spoke to Heath, he didn't wince once and was completely lucid.

Completely bloody weird.

If he's meeting up with friends, I guess he'll be okay if something does happen. I walk around to inspect my car again. I can't judge exactly how much damage there is, but there's definitely a dent.

A dent to match the one in my confused mind.

3

VERITY

I call myself a Faceless One. A drudge. Mindless job as a tech support team minion. Correct, I support the support team. I'm not allowed to offer help directly to the general public. Initially, I was, but my forthright nature didn't wash. I prefer to lose myself in fixing computer code or identifying faults anyway. Most of the guys I work with have little interest in conversation beyond swearing about client stupidity, so I stick in my world for each eight-hour shift.

My work cubicle is lost in the centre of the hive, besides two people I've worked with for the last two years. Debbie on my right, cubicle covered in family photos and her kid's drawings, and Don on my left, with his minimalist, super tidy cubicle he covers in crumbs every day when he eats the wrapped sandwich he brings from home.

My style's closer to Don's, although I've adorned my monitor with cat stickers and pinned some arty postcards to the felt-covered, boxed walls around me. I did have a stress toy to squeeze, in the shape of a dog, but I stressed the item too much and the head fell off.

I spent yesterday evening shaking and sick following my encounter with Heath, eventually distracting myself with a mini-binge on Netflix. My blog inbox held messages to answer, but not in the mood, I ignored them. I'm in touch with half a dozen people in different countries who're helping me with my latest research into the background of Alphanet executives. People who don't think I'm crazy. Last night, my brain was too fried by my encounter with Heath.

The dent in my car bumper was clearer in daylight. I'm no believer in superheroes or iron-skinned gargoyle shifters, but that's one hell of a dent. Maybe Heath's right, and my ageing car's bodywork isn't up to scratch.

The noise of a hundred conversations surrounds me, clients with telecommunication problems answered by some, those needing tech support for their new internet set up sent through to my team.

Yeah, it's a joke throughout the world, but the phrase "have you turned it off and on again?" should be framed as the company motto in the corner of the room. Second only to "have you plugged in the modem?"

Fun times.

The clock to my right, outside the glass-windowed supervisor's office, ticks closer to break time. Which department does Heath work in? He must be on this floor if he's seen me around. The fact he's seen me around and remembered me flutters my stomach because, y'know, hot guy.

After last night, I doubt he'll ever forget me.

At lunch, disappointment joins my salad as Heath doesn't appear. I sit in the lunchroom, ensuring I watch people come and go rather than keep my head in a book. Paperbacks only for me; I spend enough time staring at technology. Entertaining and dismissing the idea he's missing, or might be dead, or unconscious in hospital, I return to work.

Shift over, I tramp across the car park dreaming of the time I'll be allocated a 9 to 5 shift and not leaving work at 9:00 p.m. I parked my beaten-up car where us worker bees are allowed, away from the queens whose allocated bays are a short walk from the entrance.

"Verity!" The cultured English accent from yesterday calls my name, and I turn to Heath.

His easygoing gait shows no sign my bad driving has any long-term side effects. I halt beneath a car park spotlight at the edge. He approaches, then halts a few feet away from me, finally allowing me to see him clearly.

I blink. He's beautiful. I mean, I know that's a weird word to use about a guy, but good-looking or hot doesn't apply here. The symmetry to his face, the full mouth, the moss-green eyes fixed on mine all conspire to blank my mind. He isn't wearing a jacket today, but instead his work attire: a plain shirt stretching across his chest, with tie, trousers, and shiny shoes. The hair damp yesterday now settles around his face. I'm not big on long hair for guys, but Heath's covers his ears and reaches the top of his neck. Borderline between okay and too long for my tastes.

Ha, listen to me, like I have a chance.

He studies me in return, eyes searching mine, prickling my scalp. His eyes glisten in the twilight, and the attraction to him rises.

"Hey." I attempt to sound relaxed and end up almost squeaking.

"Sorry I missed you today, but here I am." Heath steps back, arms outstretched either side as if inviting an inspection. "Upright. Head and internal organs intact."

"Right."

"Seriously, I'm good and thanking the stars you don't drive an SUV."

"Same."

"I do have some scratches though." He indicates his arm.

"Yeah, totally unscathed wouldn't make sense." I voice out loud the thought I've carried.

"Any chance you can drop me in town? My car's in for repairs today. I scored a ride from a friend this morning but don't have...." He trails off at my wide-eyed expression. "Oh, I can call an Uber. Just thought as we're leaving at the same time you'd be happy to repay me with a ride home."

"No. I mean, yes," I say and cringe at my hasty response. "Sure. Where do you live?"

"Drop me off in town, and I'll be good. I'm meeting

some friends at the pub. Again. Usual evening." He grins, eyes crinkling in one corner. "You can join me if you like. Us."

At least *us* doesn't sound like a date, although my chest twinged at his correction. "I'm not a fan of pubs."

Heath scratches his cheek. "Right. Shame. A ride and buying me a pint would be enough compensation that I don't set my lawyers on you for damages."

"What?" I narrow my eyes and detect whether he's teasing. Lying I can spot, teasing—no.

"Kidding! So, can I?"

Jesus, he's giving me puppy-dog eyes in a face like that? *Nailed it.* Now I'm half-convinced it's me he wants to spend time with, and I waver. "Jump in. It's too bloody cold to hang around out here. I'll drop you in town, but I'll decline the offer of a drink."

Heath spends most of the journey focused on his presumably new phone, and I glance at him as we stop at the traffic lights. The yellow streetlight strokes his face I swear could be sculpted by a mischievous god. His heavy brow is pulled down, and he pulls on his bottom lip as he reads.

Rude, much?

I clear my throat, pointedly, and he looks up. "Okay?"

"We're almost there. I can drop you in the town square if that works?"

The road through the countryside switch to better lit narrow streets leading passed a small row of shops and into the tiny town centre. A statue of an ancient king is the focus of the square (the plaque with his story overwritten by graffiti tags) where teens often hang out in the evenings before the police move them on. Several pubs and small shops are opposite the square; the proliferation of pubs in the town outweighs the shops two to one.

"You sure you don't want to join us?" he asks.

"I'm driving?"

"You don't live far. Park your car and we can walk back. I'll buy you a coke."

"I don't drink caffeine this late at night."

Heath throws me a curious look. "Or juice. Or do you have someone waiting at home? Is that why you don't want to spend time with me?"

Huh? "Just my cat." Or I did; I swear he moved into my neighbour's place.

"Cat?" He pulls a face. "I promise I'll be more entertaining than a cat."

I glance at the time on my dashboard, 10:30 p.m. I haven't spent an evening out since Anna visited me from London; my best friend, I joke, abandoned me for the big city. Sometimes I wish I'd left too, enjoyed the anonymity, but I doubt I'd enjoy the noise and crazy city life invading my head. I prefer peace—and an affordable rent.

"Okay. One drink."

His face brightens. "Awesome. I just don't think you should go home yet."

Something in his words arrests me as we continue to the carpark outside my flat, as if a sad evening as a crazy cat lady isn't what he means.

Heath walks alongside me, at a distance I'd normally be oblivious to; but with him, I fight drifting across the path to attach myself to his side. Not only has he forgiven me for threatening his life, but also he's asked me to join him for an after-work drink.

If only the clones could see me now.

"What's funny?"

Heath looks down at me. Did I just snicker out loud? "Nothing. Just thinking about some friends from work."

My overactive imagination usually limits itself to theorising over which TV personality could be subtly brainwashing the masses; this time it's focused on the remote possibility Heath's interested in me.

"Do you like working at Alphanet?" he asks.

"It pays the bills."

"Isn't it boring?"

"I've been there three years now, I guess I like life staying the same."

"Hmm." Heath holds an arm out and takes my elbow guiding me around a large puddle. "I doubt I'll stay there long."

His action in saving my feet from a soaking surprises me, but not as much as the fact his hand stays against my arm a few seconds longer than needed. Close proximity to this guy sets my heart rate into overdrive and a desire for him to feel the same. Even touching me through my thin coat sparked more ideas the attraction could be mutual.

"You've only worked at the place for three weeks," I say.

"I've more interesting jobs coming up. This is just temporary."

"Moving on?"

"Probably." He glances at me. "Maybe we should make the most of the time I'm around." My eloquent response? Mouth hanging open. "If you want."

Time to turn on the lie detection. "Are you propositioning me, Heath? I only agreed to a drink at the pub!"

He halts and digs his hands into his pockets. "Do you want me to?"

Don't ask me questions like that. I clench my teeth together to stop the blunt truth coming out, and I settle on, "You're an attractive guy."

He smirks. "I know. And I'm not propositioning you. I find you intriguing. You're different."

I wrinkle my nose. The truth. Damn, a girl likes the chance of a proposition. "Are you one of us?"

His brow pulls down. "One of who?"

"You said I'm different. Intriguing. Do you know about my blog?" I stiffen. "Or are you someone who's trying to get close to me because I'm hitting on the truth."

"Wow, you're paranoid."

"Hot guys don't normally single me out for attention and tell me I'm interesting. I won't fall for that tactic." I narrow my eyes at him, and his face dimples as a smile grows.

"Their loss. And no, I'm not secret service attempting to seduce you into telling me secrets. Besides, if I wanted you to tell me the truth about something, you would."

My eyes narrow further. "Would I?"

"Ah, Verity. People can be influenced by what their name is, you know." He laughs.

"Heath? So you enjoy long walks in the countryside, then?"

His amusement drops, and he walks ahead to the pavement edge. "If you're only staying for one drink with me and my friends, we'd better be quick."

4

VERITY

The Kings Arms is the pub most popular with the locals who've never left town and spend every evening in the place. Most work dead-end jobs, one or two work here, or don't work at all.

They're here now, huddled at their usual table ensuring their pints last as long as possible, and the music matches their tastes. The younger kids, many almost half their age, steer clear; they prefer the brighter and shinier Harvester pub a couple of streets away.

One or two of them glance at me as I walk passed. I know some in the group to say hello to, but that's all.

I weave through the crammed tables, following Heath, towards a table near the back of the pub, tucked away behind a wall displaying ads for the latest designer drinks.

Two men look up and I halt, frozen, as if under a spotlight. One, spiked blond hair, welcoming smile on his face, takes a not-so-subtle look at the length of me, but the other, similar in colouring to Heath, but with messy hair, doesn't summon a smile as my accident victim introduces me.

"This is Verity. Verity, Joss and Ewan." When neither responds, he adds. "The girl from work."

"Yeah, thought so," replies the dark-haired guy, Ewan. He drops his gaze from my eyes to my mouth before looking back at me. "Hi."

Whoa. Holy hotness. When I woke up this morning, I didn't realise I'd be invited to an evening out with a delicious-guys smorgasbord. Maybe I should run down guys more often. They look as if they share Heath's height, and certainly his build. And looks. *Ah, crap, I'm staring.* What the hell is with me that I can go from considering whether I should proposition Heath before he leaves to considering what's underneath his friends' shirts? Lack of sex life and too many hormones, that's what.

"Call me Vee."

"Hey, Vee," says Joss and smiles. *Ouch. More dimples.*

And no girls? I count the chairs at the table. Only two extra.

"No girls," says Joss and I snap my head round as he grins at me. "Easy to read people's minds sometimes."

Ewan flashes him a look, but Joss immediately drops an arm across his shoulder. "And much as I love these guys, our relationship is perfectly platonic."

I cross my arms at his unnecessary need to indicate he's interested in girls. Ewan shrugs Joss's arm away and picks up his pint glass. "But not always friendly," he mutters.

When Joss pinches his cheek, I fight a smile. Either Ewan's a grumpy drunk or isn't as friendly as Joss would like.

Heath plonks himself on the stool next to Joss, leaving the seat besides Ewan the only one vacant. Oh great. I sit stiffly and shift my stool away from Ewan, catching sight of an impressive tattooed bicep beneath his black T-shirt. My attempt to move the seat surreptitiously fails as Ewan laughs softly in my direction.

Heath disappears to the bar to buy a round of drinks, and I clasp my hands in my lap under the table, as the tension thickens around us.

"Do you live in Grangeton?" I ask, grasping for polite conversation.

"Near here," replies Ewan.

Conversation closed down, I delve around for something else, but I'm interrupted by Joss. "So you're the girl who ran Heath down last night?"

I fight the heat crossing my cheeks. "Yes. And I have no excuse."

Joss blows air into his cheeks. "That's one hell of a way to get a guy's attention."

"Or a girl's," puts in Ewan. "Not many guys would throw themselves in front of a car so she'd notice him."

"Very funny. It wasn't deliberate; I didn't see Heath. It's not my fault he was loitering near my house."

"Was he?" Joss straightens. "He must really want to see you."

“I was kidding. Don't make him sound weird," says Ewan.

"I live in the town centre, nothing unusual about Heath passing," I say as much to myself as them.

But my heart thumps at the thought this wasn't a coincidence, especially considering his hints he wants to spend time with me.

"A bit weird he wasn't hurt," I reply and watch for their reaction.

Joss shrugs. "You've seen him. Solid guy. Reckon you'd need to hit him hard to do any damage. He says you only bumped him."

Only bumped him? He was lying in the freaking road.

"Well, he's okay and that's what matters," says Ewan.

Did Heath plan this, and if he did, why has he invited me to also spend time with two other men? I need to finish the drink when it arrives and get out of here. However friendly they are, I'm not sure I want to end up in a position that involves me alone with them all.

What if they *all* follow me home?

I swallow down my nerves. My paranoia's out of hand recently: thinking I'm being followed, Heath hinting he knows about my research.

"What's happening?" Heath places our two drinks on the table. "Is Joss teasing you?"

"Just telling lovely Verity about your secret crush that caused you to pursue her across town."

"Screw you," he mutters and sits beside me. "Sorry about my friend."

"Hey, at least I'm not hitting on her!" says Joss with a laugh.

"Oh, she wouldn't know what hit her if you did," replies Heath.

Ewan snorts and Joss pulls a “ha ha” face.

I pick up my glass and stare at the contents. "You're making her uncomfortable," replies Ewan and nods at me.

His concern surprises me, and I sip my sparkling apple juice. How slowly do I need to drink this before I can leave but not seem rude? Heath sits beside me, and I'm sandwiched between the pair. I hold my breath. God, don't let either of them brush my arm, leg, anything because this effect is freaking me out.

"Listen, I invited Verity tonight as a thanks for giving me a ride from work tonight. I didn't realise you were in full-blown-asshole mode." He looks at me apologetically. "I'm sorry if we're making you uncomfortable. We kind of... banter."

"Or argue," puts in Joss.

"Long-term friends, I'm guessing," I say. "If you're behaving like this together."

"A few years, yeah." Ewan drinks.

"Maybe Verity could invite some friends next time? Make it less uncomfortable?" asks Joss, raising a brow. Of the pair, I can't stop looking at Joss, and not only because he's friendlier to me. His relaxed attitude and stomach-flipping smile draw me towards him. Do they have a magic ability to attract girls?

If the hypothetical—and a hundred percent unlikely to happen—situation arose, I do not know who I'd choose between Joss and Heath.

See, crazy hormones?

“Maybe," I say with a bright smile, knowing full well I don't have any friends I could introduce them to.

Which means I could keep them all to myself.

I smirk at my thought. Joss clears his throat, and when I look up, he tips his head and fights a smile.

My glass empties at what I hope is a respectable pace and conversation switches to general talk about everything from what it's like to live here for years, to the last best meal we ate. I glean little about the trio apart from they've known each other three years, Joss works part-time at a hotel, and Ewan is “something to do with computers,” and that they share a house.

I gradually relax around them, as if I've met with old friends after years now the suggestive comments have stopped. I've missed socialising, and they're intersecting to be around. I'm tired and need to leave, but there's something else persuading me to stay. Each guy has a weird, but different, effect on me. I’m curious about the Ewan hidden behind his taciturn reaction to me and by Joss's opposite friendly nature, and how he looks at me as if seeing into my mind. Heath’s effect is stronger as we’ve interacted more, but this doesn’t stop me wanting to do the same with the others.

I grab my hoodie from the seat beside me and stand. "Thanks for the drink."

Heath and Joss look at each other as I shove an arm into the jacket.

"Already?" asks Heath.

"I said just one."

"Take her home," puts in Ewan in a low voice.

"I'm fine," I say and smile though his comment sounded like a command.

"The weather isn't great," Ewan retorts. "What if you have an accident? Hit someone again?"

At this Joss can barely contain his mirth. I shoot a

look at him, and he bites down on his lip, them mouths “sorry.”

"I'm walking," I say through gritted teeth.

"Are you sure you don't want to stay for another and more of our scintillating conversation?" Heath stands. "I'll buy."

"No. It's fine."

Nobody speaks and weirdness seeps back into the situation, as I picture the three of them frogmarching me out of the pub and accompanying me home.

"I'll walk you home, at least," says Heath.

Hmm. "Okay."

I say my goodbyes to Joss and Ewan; Joss waves and Ewan nods, and I'm relieved when only Heath walks into the night with me.

My breath mists as we head back towards my place, relieved the rain stopped. All the way back, I waver between do I invite him in or do I not? He doesn't speak as we walk. Is he thinking the same?

"Thanks for an interesting evening," I say as we reach outside my flat.

"I'd rather you stayed longer." He inclines his head to the building. "Don't worry, I won't ask you to invite me in. I just wanted to see you were safe."

I nod through my disappointment as he pulls out his phone. "Can I give you my number? In case you want to contact me?"

"Sure."

Heath holds his hand out, and I place mine in his palm. He types, long fingers sweeping the screen and hands it back.

I stare blankly at the phone. Heath steps backwards

into the car park and looks from side to side. What's he looking for?

My stomach flips as Heath reaches out and takes hold of my jacket collar in both hands and tugs it closer around me, looking down with curiosity in his eyes. For one heart-stopping moment I think I'm about to receive a good night kiss. "Take care, Verity."

"I will."

As he walks back into the evening, what sticks with me the most isn't his almost kiss, or the fact he never asked for my phone number, but the earnestness in his voice when he told me I should take care.

5

VERITY

I tread carefully across the moss-covered pavers slippery after the recent rain. There're two doors to reach my flat, one at street level that opens to a narrow staircase and another at the top of the stairs and above the shop. Both are deadlocked, although the doors themselves aren't as sturdy as I'd prefer.

Initially, I shared this place with Anna. After she left, I expected to be lonely or uncomfortable alone but never have been. I prefer my own space, as did Anna, so our flat share was harmonious. Crime rates are low in town, but two doors between me and the outside world helps with feeling secure.

I carefully bolt the downstairs door behind me, then tramp up the concrete steps leading to the flat. As I place a hand on the scratched black door handle, the lever moves down.

Did I forget to lock up?

I pause, listening for movement inside. Nothing. Heath was on my mind this morning, for a number of reasons. Did that distract me, why I forgot to lock the door? I slowly lower the handle and push open the unlocked door.

What the fuck?

Every book that was on my shelf is now on the floor, across the table or piled on the sofa. I have dozens, and not a single one remains on the shelf. I halt, keys in hand, one pushed between my fingers ready to use as a weapon in case the book-trashing home invader is still inside.

No sound. There're few places to hide because the living area in my small flat's open plan the kitchen's at the far end of the lounge area. Front door still open, I tread into the room, pushing books to one side with my shoes. Have they taken anything? The kitchen drawers are closed and the rest of the room appears untouched. I stare at my TV. Why didn't whoever broke in take that?

A door to the rear of the room leads to my bedroom—and it's closed. Fear coils around my stomach and tightens, my imagination running wild. I should leave.

Instead, idiocy takes over. I summon the courage to open the door and my shoulders drop in relief when the room contains nothing and nobody, apart from my unmade bed and small nightstand. To be sure, I flick the light switch.

Who the hell would trash my place?

Grumbling, I head back to pick up some books while

my mind jumps from option to option. First up, call the police.

The door slams and I spin around, gripping the paperback, adrenaline launching into my blood.

A man stands between me and the door. He's taller than any I've seen before, wiry frame beneath a leather jacket and tight jeans, older than me. His hair's blue, spiked at the front, but the unusual colour isn't what strikes me.

The eyes staring back at me are violet. Not flecks, but full on violet irises.

Neither of us moves or speaks, but the man keeps his hand on the door. I run my eyes over him. No weapons. Not visible ones, anyway. I grip the paperback tighter and focus on staying calm as I back towards the kitchen area.

"Hello, Verity. How are you?" The man's voice is low, almost a whisper, with a hint of accent I can't catch.

"What are you doing in my flat?" I continue to back up, mind jumping around. Self-defence. Book? Sharp knife in kitchen drawer.

"I came for you."

Time stills as my chest tightens. Fuck. "Don't touch me!"

The weird guy steps further into my home, closer to me. "I won't hurt you if you walk out of this place with me, I promise."

My truth detector tells me he doesn't intend to do anything right now, but after we leave? "I'm not going anywhere with you."

"You are. Somebody I know needs to talk to you, and it's a matter of some urgency."

"Who?"

"Come on, Verity." He beckons me towards him with one pale hand.

"No! Leave before I call the police!" I pull my phone from my pocket and Heath's number's still onscreen from earlier.

Heath? I bloody wish I hadn't waited for him to walk out of sight before coming into my flat.

And doubly wish I'd invited him in.

I begin to dial, but pale dude focuses his eyes on the phone and the metal heats beneath my fingers. With a yelp, I drop the phone to the floor where it bounces across the tiles.

A livid burn appears in the palm of my hand. "What the fuck?" I say through gritted teeth.

"Nice place you have here." I stare in disbelief between my hand and him, as he leans against the door, ankles crossed. "You like candles, I see."

My confusion grows as he inclines his head to the pillar candles on the table; the scented ones I use to disguise the damp smell in the place.

"Did you know candles are a leading cause of house fires?" He steps forward and picks one up, as I eye the door for an escape route, caressing my sore palm.

"Leave my flat," I say in an attempt at a brave voice.

"Wiring too."

"What?"

"Wiring in old homes isn't always up to scratch. A big cause of electric fires." He watches as I shuffle towards the phone on the carpet and steps between me and the phone. "Don't touch that. It's hot."

Fuck this. I can't get passed him to my front door, but no way is he touching me.

I snatch the phone from the floor, ignoring the scalding heat and charge into my bedroom. Heart pounding blood in my ears, I slam closed, and lean against, the door. Why can't this have a lock too?

Then I groan. *Dumbass.* I should've run to the bathroom where I could lock myself in.

"Verity!" The man's tone switches from mocking to irritated, and the handle on the door moves next to me.

I push my body harder against the wood and swap my phone from hand to hand as if holding a hot potato. Heat sears again, growing unbearable, and I drop the phone to the floor.

What do I do if I can't call for help?

The handle stops moving, and the flat grows quiet for a few moments. My bedroom window overlooks the street and climbing out would be a two-storey drop to the tarmac.

A loud pop noise and flash of light stutters my heart as the lightbulb above me blows. Another pop and I jerk in surprise again. Scorch marks surround the empty wall socket to my right. The noise repeats all around and with it the smell of burnt plastic.

"I wouldn't stay in there, Verity," calls the man.

Before I can answer, flames shoot through the broken light fitting and ignite the curtains, blocking any possibility I can escape that way. The orange illuminates the room and licks the wall, towards the carpet. When they reach, a fiery trail paves straight towards me.

The terror freezes my mind and body, mesmerised by

the flames. How long do I have before my whole home ignites? Like a rabbit smoked out of a hole, I fling open the door and head back into the other room, aiming for the front door. The man is back to resting there with a sardonic grin on his face. "Changed your mind? Coming with me?"

"I need to get out and call 999! My home is on fire!" I shout.

He sneers. "Hence, it will be a good idea to leave. With me."

My instinct is to rush him and the door, but in my panic, I can't move. There's a strange aura around him, and I might be insane, but I'd swear he isn't human. The slant to his violet eyes, the unnatural paleness of his skin... Alien? I've come across enough conspiracy theories in my digging to believe in alien life. Is he about to beam me up to the mothership? *Omigod, are insane thoughts the best I can do in this situation?*

"Do you need some extra persuasion?" He lifts one hand and clicks his fingers, stepping away from the door. "My friend's waiting outside in case you didn't cooperate."

The man's mouth twists, and I hear thudding behind him as somebody climbs the stairs. The violet-eyed guy steps away just in time for him to avoid the door as it's flung open.

Someone fills the entrance, head almost touching the frame, as he looks at me with stone cold eyes in a face that looks like someone hit him repeatedly with a frying pan. His broad shoulders and muscles make his neck seem non-existent, torso solid and the widest I've seen since being grossed out watching body builders on TV.

I don't have time to register anything else before the hideous man advances towards me. I back up again, ass hitting the wall. I gasp as his cool fingers curl around my neck, long fingernails pressing into my skin. Grey eyes stare into mine, and his scent turns my stomach and dizzies me, pungent like rotting flesh, mingling with the burning smell emanating from my bedroom.

I choke against his hold as he squeezes my windpipe, and I flail my arms in an attempt to get a grip on and pull him off me. As if I'd have the chance against him.

"You can't drag me out of here unconscious," I rasp, turning my face to the tall man, standing with his arms crossed.

"Nobody will see."

"Of course they will! My flat's above a shop in the middle of the town. There're people passing close by."

"Nobody will see," he repeats, voice firm.

My attacker's face changes, shimmering the way a channel on TV does when trying to bring a picture into focus. I choke a scream as, instead of a human face, a nightmare visage almost touches mine. His skin reddens, the grey eyes blackening, spreading from the irises into the whites of his eyes. The hold on my neck's joined by a stinging sensation, as if I'm being stung by a hive of bees.

My strangled scream erupts as his mouth opens and stars cross my eyes, accompanying an inky blackness as the grip tightens. The door behind him flings open and a figure appears.

"Fuck!" the figure shouts.

My eyes widen in shock and relief.

Heath.

Eyes on me, he extends a hand to the right and flicks

his fingers. A flash of white light throws from the tips, hitting the tall guy square in the chest who stumbles backwards. His eyes glow brightly, body stiffening before he falls to the floor without a sound.

Heath launches himself at my assailant, who hasn't reacted to Heath's arrival, instead focused on choking me. The man's eyes, still on mine, widen for a second, his reflexes not fast enough to counter the attack from behind. Mouth parting, a gasp escapes his lips, fingers loosening on my neck. As his hand slips along my skin, he crumples downwards to the floor, with an inhuman yell.

Clutching my neck, I stare down at the carved wooden handle of a knife stuck into his back. Heath immediately yanks the knife from the guy's back and approaches the man on the floor. He kicks him with a booted toe and swears again under his breath. Bile rises in my throat as Heath lifts a knife and plunges it with force into his chest.

I slump against the wall and stare ahead, dizzy from the shock and pain, as Heath crouches down and extends a hand to touch my neck. I wince; my skin stings beneath his fingertips.

In my head, I scream "what the fuck?" but my body involuntarily shakes, throat too tight to speak, as Heath withdraws his fingers.

"You'll be okay," he says and strokes a hand down my hair. "I told you, we should've stayed at the pub." He looks around, unflustered for a guy who just brutally murdered another guy. Two guys. Were they guys? Oh god, please let me wake up. "Are you okay?"

I blink at him, watching the knife, momentarily

worried he'll use it on me too after I witnessed his murderous rampage. "My flat's on fire," I croak out.

My words jerk him out of his concerned look. "What? Shit. Where?" I point towards my room with shaking hands. "Bloody fae asshole." Heath opens his jacket and slides the knife into his front pocket. "Right. Let's go."

"With you?"

Heath holds out a hand to help me to my feet. "Unless you want to hang out in a burning flat." I hesitate. "Verity? Seriously? Fire will hurt you a damn sight more than I will."

"Right." I grab his hand. Strong fingers curl around mine, and he pulls me to my feet as if I weigh nothing more than a small child. A strange strength buzzes into my limbs, fuelling energy and soothing some of the panic. I sway and steady myself against his chest.

"Get out. There're more coming," he says, stepping away from my touch.

I stiffen. "More who? Where?"

"Demons. Fuck. Leave now."

"What do you mean d—" I'm interrupted as Heath half-drags me out of my splintered front door, and I trip down the stone stairs behind him. A white SUV is parked next to mine, and the lights flash as Heath unlocks the door.

"Get in."

"Where are we going?"

"Please, just get in before more of the fae's buddies arrive." He yanks open the passenger door.

"My flat...."

He huffs and drags out his phone. "Don't worry, I'll sort this. Just get in the car. We need to go. Now." Heath jumps into the car as he dials; I climb into the SUV and belt myself in.

I don't know what the hell is going on here, but the orange glow in my bedroom window and two men dead on my lounge floor isn't a good end to my day.

6

VERITY

The lit town streets switch to darker country lanes as Heath speeds away from my home. For a few minutes, neither of us speaks. I sit on my cold hands, attempting to catch up to what's happening.

Heath's phone rings and he answers over speaker.

"Did you find her?" asks a voice. "Is she okay?"

He side glances me. "Yeah. I'm bringing her back."

"Back where?" I ask. "Who's that?"

"Hey, Verity, it's Joss," calls a voice. "How's things?"

"Oh, you know, a man apparently called Fay tried to abduct me and set fire to my house."

The sound of snorted laughter comes down the line. "Fay, huh? Is that right, Heath?"

"Yeah. Not fucking funny, he had a bodyguard with

him. Now deceased. Told you they'd located her. We should've found and spoken to her before they did."

"Her is sitting next to you," I retort.

"Sorry. Verity."

"Vee."

"I like Vee," puts in Joss. "Single letter names, awesome people."

"What happened to the fae?" A second voice comes across the speakers, and even without seeing his sullen face, I can guess who this is. Ewan.

"Dead."

"Oh, shit, man," complains Ewan. "Seriously?"

"His fucking demon was attacking Verity! I don't know if they're intending to kill her or what."

"Heath. They can't kill her if you're around. You know that."

"I panicked, okay?" he snaps back.

"But you can't go around killing fae, for fuck's sake! Now they've an extra reason not to trust us. Nice work," replies Ewan with a snarl to his voice.

"Next time something needs dealing with, you bloody go then!"

"This would be easier if Xander hadn't upped and disappeared again. He's better at this shit," replies Joss. "Have you heard from him?"

"No. He never contacts me first if we argue. You know that. Look, I'm almost home, can we talk then?" Heath turns the SUV down a narrow lane, the tree canopies above us folding over the road and meeting, obscuring the stars.

"And nobody's following you?" asks Joss.

"Not as far as I know."

"S'okay, I have the place on lockdown. Any of those guys feet touch our ground, their hair will fall out and skin turn grey." Ewan snickers to himself. "And we all know fae will want to avoid that."

This is weird. Really bloody odd. Heath told me his car was at the garage and couldn't be driven, and suddenly it's outside my house. I toyed with the idea of leaping from the car at the first set of traffic lights in town, then hightailing it to the police station, but something about the situation I just escaped, and Heath's actions, suggest I'm better off around him.

Apart from the fact he's a knife-wielding, homicidal guy.

"Where did you come from?" I ask him. "You left."

"Yeah, I came back."

"Obviously," I mutter. "Did you know that was going to happen?"

"Suspected but thought you were safe when I left you." He slams his palm on the steering wheel. "Fuck! I should've got to the bastards before they touched you."

"You're going to tell me I'll be safe with you, aren't you?" I ask him.

He glances at me, then back to the road. "I was, but thought it would sound like a cliche and you'd decide I was abducting you. But it's true. You're safer when the five of us are together."

"Five?"

"Yeah, you met three of us. One is on a kind of mission, I guess."

"Like you? What the hell just happened? Who was that?"

Heath doesn't respond for a few moments. "I know it's

a big ask, but will you stay the night with us? We'll talk. Then you can decide what you want to do."

A large farmhouse house looms towards us, beyond the trees, and Heath stops the SUV in front of a low metal gate attached to a chain fence. He hops out and pulls open the gate. When he drives through and closes the gate again, I wait for the trepidation to swirl into my system as we approach.

Instead, I experience a strange calm the closer we get to the large brick house. Heath parks the SUV beside a large motorcycle. When he walks out and opens my door, I hesitate. Heath digs his hands in his pockets as he regards me.

"If you want to leave, that's okay, I'll take you to a hotel or a friend's. But I hope you understand why you'll be safer here. There're more like him out there who want to find you, and I can't guarantee you'll be safe alone tonight."

I follow Heath and his cryptic words into the house. The slate floors and low, wooden-beamed ceilings add a rustic feel, and the place is warm. A pungent herb smell permeates the building; I recognise cloves and maybe sage? We walk through the large hallway and into a kitchen with a large, rectangular pine table. Joss and Ewan look up from where they're studying a laptop on the table in front of Ewan.

"Good evening, Vee. Again." Joss's natural smile and warmth contrast with Ewan's sullenness and Heath's guarded nature, and I wish he'd been the one to find me tonight. Maybe they leave the killing to Heath?

I tuck my hands under my arms.

"You don't look too good," Joss says.

The shaking runs through my body again as his words remind me what happened. "I... Something... Heath just..." I wrap my arms tighter around myself, as if this will stop me collapsing to the floor.

Joss stands and crosses to the sink to fill a glass with water. He passes it to me, the concern in his eyes blooming warmth in my chest. Heath remained edgy on the journey here, understandably, and I need this friendlier face.

The kitchen's brighter than the pub was, and I take a closer look at Joss's features. His eyes are the same green as Heath's, the perfect bone structure and symmetry too. He's slimmer than Heath, and although I guess they're the same age, he has the air of someone older and calmer.

This guy towers over me like Heath too. If it weren't for his calm demeanour, I'd be wary of the strength I can see in him.

He returns the steady gaze. "Are you hurt?" He gestures at me. "Your neck's red. Did he do anything else?" I swear he's about to touch my throat, but instead he nods at me.

"Nothing, apart from set fire to my bedroom."

"He was in your bedroom?" Joss cocks a brow. "I know they're seductive, but that was bloody quick work on his part."

"Who're seductive? And no, *I* was in the bedroom hiding from him. And did you miss the 'on fire' part?"

Joss rubs his cheek. "Smart move getting away. They're vicious buggers."

"I kind of noticed that," I retort.

Heath pulls out a chair and gestures to me. "She's in shock. Vee, sit down."

I obey, clutching my water. Ewan hasn't paid me much attention, instead his focus remaining on scrolling through the laptop screen, messy hair disguising his expression.

"Who was it?" asks Ewan.

"Not sure. Fae definitely, but not someone I've come across."

"If he had a demon with him, I doubt he's allied with the Council," replies Joss.

"Xander told you something was happening behind the scenes with them, that they're hiding this from us," replies Ewan.

"Yes, and that's where Xander has gone, right?" asks Heath.

"With his own personal brand of diplomacy," says Joss with a laugh.

"More diplomatic than killing people, huh, Heath?" Ewan slams the laptop lid closed. "Idiot."

"What would you've done?" snaps Heath. "I couldn't stop myself. Literally, saw her and had no control over anything but getting Verity out of there."

Joss and Ewan exchange glances. "Xander was right. The Fifth equals trouble."

"I'm sure everything will be okay once she's strong enough," Heath replies.

"Strong enough for what?" I ask. "Somebody please tell me what's happening? Why are you talking about demons?" Despite my scrambled head, their words resounded, the extraordinariness of their conversation edging reality after what I saw.

"How open-minded are you about the world?" asks Heath.

Joss burst into laughter. "She's a conspiracy theorist. She's open-minded about a lot of things." He bites his lip. "Not everything."

"I'm not a conspiracy theorist. Don't use that phrase."

"We've seen your blog. It's how we found you," says Joss.

"Yeah, broadcasting yourself around the world," mutters Ewan. "Not smart."

"She doesn't know! And it meant we found her too," replies Heath.

"What don't I know?"

"You investigate shit. Some would call it obsessive paranoia, but we're looking into the same things as you. Government. Corporate. Someone's pulling the strings."

I straighten. "Yes! Exactly. Money's exchanging hands. Whoever's controlling the world has a reach into all society."

"Nobody's controlling the world," remarks Ewan. "They're trying, but we're going to stop them."

"Oh!" The situation dawns on me. "Are you the guys I spoke to the other week? The ones who've been emailing me about the new CEO of Alphanet and his connection to the British government?"

Now it's Ewan's turn to straighten. "No. Who's contacted you?"

"A guy who works for them. He wanted to meet me. Our group is by invite only and have a code, you know, on the secret boards we use, so I know he's genuine. He has information."

"Your secret boards are filled with lunatics," says Ewan. "Do you mean Spillz?"

Is Ewan a secret member of our site in the deep web? We're all anonymous on there and share a passion for hacking into or digging for evidence. "No, DoomMan."

He frowns. "I haven't heard of or looked into him." Ewan reopens the laptop, lips pursed as he taps the keys.

"He could be fae?" suggests Heath. "Or from the Order?" I look from guy to guy, increasingly losing track of their rapid conversation. "You did right not to meet him."

"Ah. I kind of arranged to," I admit.

Joss's face darkens. "On your own?"

"In a public place!" I retort.

"That doesn't always help," Heath says.

I place my elbows on the table and run hands through my hair. "This is exhausting. Please tell me what's happening. Why did someone break into my flat and attempt to barbecue me? I should be contacting the police, not sitting here!"

The men fall silent, and I try hard not to keep my eyes off Joss. I've never had a thing for blond guys, but each time I look over, his eyes are on me. His presence calms me, but there's a contradiction in that the way he looks at me stirs a desire for him to touch me.

"Do you believe there's more to the world than humans?" asks Joss in a soft voice.

"I've always considered alien life is a safe bet," I reply. "I mean the universe is infinite, right? How can we be the only planet that can sustain a population?"

"Yeah, but other things. Like witches. Demons." He pauses. "Vampires. Fae."

"I know Wiccans."

Ewan snorts and doesn't look up from his laptop. "Not the religion. A different kind of witches."

Snarky, much? "Demons? I'm not religious. Ghosts, maybe. Vampires? Well, probably some weird cults who drink blood. I've heard of that."

"You're not religious?" asks Heath. "Really?"

"I have a thing about not believing people. I hate lies. I read the Bible—forcibly—at school, and as soon as the teacher discussed it, she really annoyed me. She was supposed to teach me, not lie to me with stories invented to keep the masses in check."

"Ha!" Joss laughs and points at me. "Absolutely! But that's the thing with stories, right? They get told through generations over hundreds of years, until someone writes them down. The stories stem from somewhere though. It's a version of the truth, right? The original truth became lost in people's motivations to control others. The original messages are lost. Doesn't mean there's no Higher Power out there, or that you should ignore the morality taught."

I smile. "That was always my opinion, although I don't believe in God and the devil."

"But demons are real," Joss bats back and our smiles disappear. "You just met one."

Mine doesn't disappear because he's lying, but because, thanks to my oh-so awesome talents, I know, in no uncertain terms, he's telling me the truth.

A truth that cannot possibly be true.

"What?" I ask in a low voice.

"And vampires and shifters and fae and—"

"Zombies?" I interrupt sarcastically.

Ewan snorts again, which I take as a derisive no. But my heart's speeding at each word, and suddenly my exhaustion's replaced by energy suggesting I run.

Every. Word. Is. True.

"I think you should stop there, Joss," says Heath. "Vee's had a pretty shit evening, and I don't think a run down on the secret world living alongside the human is the best conversation right now."

"I get that, but she's confused. I think Vee needs to understand that she's in danger from something, and the police can't and won't help her with it."

"Why won't the police help? Someone committed arson in my home and attacked me!"

"If the Order are in government and corporations, do you really think law enforcement is exempt?" asks Ewan.

On everything I've heard today, this confirmation of my suspicions over the last few years smacks me the hardest. "What Order?"

"The one you investigate but don't have a name for. Vee, you already suspected that."

"Fuck," I mumble.

"I'll give you my phone if you want to contact the police or anybody else," says Heath. "But I'd rather you waited and considered the safest thing to do. Honestly, giving yourself over to the police is not safe." He pauses. "You're exhausted, I can see that. Stay. Sleep. We can talk again tomorrow."

"Yeah. I told the guys you could have my bed." Joss nods at me. "Don't worry. I won't climb into it with you."

"Can you stop with the innuendo," mutters Ewan. "She's in a house with three guys she hardly knows. Do you want her to freak out and leave?"

"Ah, sorry, Vee. I don't mean anything by my comments. Just teasing you."

For the first time tonight, I know he's lying to me because I've seen the opposite in his eyes.

I'm hesitant when Joss offers to show me where I can sleep. Thoughts of demons and God-knows what waiting for me in the night, and conformation of my own suspicions about whether I can trust the police, sway me towards staying. The calmness in Joss I've picked up on since I arrived intensifies the more he speaks to me, or the closer he gets. In an odd way, spending time with the three guys feels like meeting up with old friends.

The stairs to the second storey are worn from years of use, and at the top, a wide hallway leads to several rooms. Joss pauses by a door and rubs the back of his head as he indicates the room.

"Your accommodation for the night, ma'am."

I shake my head at his mock formality, and he grins. Joss flicks a switch, and I peek into the room. A large bed fills the room, with a small wardrobe in one corner and heavy curtains across the window. Bare. Functional. Apart from clothes spread around the room, which Joss walks in and collects in his arms.

"Ah yeah, sorry. I'll move these."

"I'm fine to sleep on the sofa," I say.

"No. You need to rest after the day you've had."

I swallow and sit on the edge of the bed. "If I can."

Concern crosses Joss's face, and he sets the clothes on

a nearby chair before sitting next to me. The mattress sinks as he does, and his leg touches mine. My first instinct is to move my leg away, but his accidental touch has a weird combination of effects. Hyperawareness this man close to me digs into the primal part of my brain, triggering a sudden arousal, and then it's replaced by a soothing drop into comfort.

I turn to him as the remaining reticence I had about staying here drops away. His green eyes meet mine, and my pulse rate kicks up a notch again at the affection and concern in them. Joss bites his lip and shifts away so we're no longer touching.

"You all have the same eye colour," I say.

"You have green eyes too."

People occasionally comment on the striking colour, and I'd noticed Heath's, but how many people can look at someone else and realise they share the same shade?

"Are we related?" I ask him. "Is that what this is?"

"We're not blood, apart from Xander and Heath; they're brothers."

"Right." I pick at the dark grey sheets I sit on. "My head hurts."

"Do you feel any calmer?" asks Joss.

"I do, maybe the prospect of a comfortable bed and the protection of three guys helps." I give a wry smile. "Thanks for giving me your room."

Joss shrugs and reaches out to touch my hand before stopping and sitting on both instead. "All good. I want you to feel you belong."

"So, yeah. Maybe I should sleep?"

He stands at my pointed comments and picks up his

clothes. "Good plan. And I promise not to reclaim my bed while you're sleeping in it."

"You'd regret it if you tried," I warn him.

"Vee, I hope you realise I'm kidding. I have no intention of doing anything inappropriate."

I laugh at his use of the word inappropriate. “I know. I can tell."

"Ah, the human lie detector, of course you can." He walks backwards towards the door and gives a small bow as he leaves. "Sleep well. You're safe here."

I watch as he quietly closes the door before flopping backwards on the bed and staring at the bare light bulb overhead.

Again, he's telling the truth.

7

VERITY

If only sleeping in a stranger's bed was the strangest thing that happened to me last night. The sheets were clean, but the room held the lingering scent similar to but different from Heath's, like sandalwood. I buried my nose into the pillow, soothed by the scent and imagining the man with his arms around me. My semiconscious dreams wandered into less soothing directions and I jerked awake, disgusted with myself at the way they headed.

Why do I feel protected here when these three men are entangled in a crazy world I'm being dragged into?

I slept with the lamp on, something I haven't done since I was a child. Since the demons I once imagined under my bed are real, I'm inclined to stay in the light.

I'm unsure how long I perched on the edge of the bed,

grasping onto the reality I'd left behind. I understand Heath not wanting every question and answer dealt with while I'm in shock and tired, but my biggest question is what has this to do with me? What makes a supernatural duo decide they want to abduct a tech support worker from Grangeton? Probably the same reason a trio of smoking hot guys have all their attention focused on me.

I have nothing but the clothes I arrived in, along with an impetus to return home and find out what mess is left. Dragging my hands through my thick brown hair, I make my way to the kitchen.

Joss sits at the table, toast in one hand and phone in the other. The sun through the kitchen window picks out golden highlights in his hair, and I can't help the heat surging inside my belly. He looks up, the green eyes that match his friends' filled with a warmth to match his smile. Joss sets the phone down beside his plate.

"Morning, Verity, how are you?"

"Vee. And confused. I need to go home and see what the place is like and if it's uninhabitable. I bloody hope my stuff isn't all burned." I gesture at my clothes. "Thank god it's the weekend and I don't need to head to work in the same clothes as yesterday."

"Sure. One of us will take you home to collect some things."

Collect? "I don't know if I'm staying."

"Because I told you about demons and vampires?"

He fixes me with his look of truth and my stomach surges for a different reason. Maybe the truth I'm reading in him is his belief and not reality.

But his friends didn't chastise him for teasing me.

"No, because I hardly know you."

"Who else are you going to stay with?"

He looks back at his phone. Good point. I grit my teeth against my narrowing options. Hotels are expensive and could come with added demon.

I shift from foot to foot. "Um, Joss. Where do you keep your coffee? I'd like a cup."

"Oh shit, sorry." He stands and rakes a hand through his hair. "I'm not used to visitors."

The pursed lips and vulnerable edge softens me against his actions. There's something about a thoughtful guy with a softer side that sucks me in.

"Right. Coffee's here. Instant, I'm afraid. Milk in fridge. Do you want toast?" He opens cupboards and the fridge, dragging out items required for breakfast, and I smile at his fussing.

"Your house is very clean," I say, looking around the spotless kitchen. There aren't even any fingermarks on the stainless steel fridge. "Especially for a bunch of guys."

"Yeah, Ewan's a bit of a clean freak. Are you sure you're not hungry? I can make you something."

I shake my head and watch as he spoons instant coffee into a large blue mug. "Can I ask you something too?"

"I imagine you have a lot you want to ask." He turns and rests against the kitchen bench, long legs outstretched.

Joss wears a plain grey T-shirt today, with black jeans. The muscle definition across his chest and strong biceps barely covered by the sleeves distract me. An image of stroking the fine blond down on his arms flutters into my mind and I push it away. Following last night's revelations and some of the reactions he has to me too, I'm unsure if he's a mind reader. And if he is, I don't want him coming across unclean thoughts.

"Who are you?" I ask.

"Joss. Smith."

I splutter. "Smith? Really?"

"Am I lying?"

I pout at his knowing look. "No. And how do you know I can tell if you are or not?"

"Firstly, most people would've told me I was lying about demons and shit last night. Second, I know it's your thing."

"Thing," I laugh.

He shrugs. "I have one too. I detect people's emotions." He pauses. "So it means I can detect when inhuman creatures are around too. Soulless ones whose emotions are limited to hunger, lust, and anger." The kettle clicks off. "How do you have your coffee? White?"

His switch from the extraordinary to the mundane catches me off guard. "White. Two sugars."

"Aww, seriously? But you're sweet enough."

I roll my eyes at his comment but he remains serious. "I'm not lying, you're cuter than I expected."

I really wish I had not imagined this man naked in his bed with me last night. Okay, that was excusable because it was my subconscious and not deliberate. Right?

"Stop flirting and tell me what you mean about 'my thing.'" And creatures and demons and *hell* what will they tell me next?

"Your name, I'm sure you made the connection. You're Verity."

"Yes, ironic."

"No, you're *Verity*. Y'know. The word. Truth."

"Yes," I repeat. "I know the definition."

"No, you don't get it." He stirs the coffee and drops the spoon in the sink. "You're obsessed with the truth, aren't you? You're delving into the lies woven around the world that blinds people with ignorance."

This personality trait fits my name, absolutely, and I stick to Vee mostly these days. I don't like people knowing my full name; I never liked it.

"Kind of. I know you were telling the truth about the paranormal world last night, or you believe you are."

"Oh, I am." Joss passes me the cup and his fingertips brush mine. A sensation triggers along my arm, buzzing through, similar to Heath's touch yesterday. I hastily lift the cup to my lips and sip.

Joss's eyes darken, and I almost spill my coffee when he cups my cheek. "There's a lot you need to know, but here's the most important. I'm going to look after you."

Considering the amount of heart racing in the last 24 hours, I'm going to end up with medical problems. And this? I've always been the “strong woman who doesn't need a man,” from car maintenance to assorted DIY jobs, but the words tighten my stomach. He's earnest, and I don't need to sense the truth this time.

"Like Heath did?" I say.

Joss drops his hand and frowns. "He was the one who needed to be there last night, although we didn't expect him to be that reckless."

An image of the man with the knife in his back flashes, and the guys' annoyance Heath killed the violet-eyed man. "What are fae?" I ask. "I've heard the word but don't know about them, like I do vampires and werewolves."

"The fae are one of the supernatural races who live side by side with humans. Their realm was being destroyed, and the fae were dying as their magic faded, so they crossed over to your world. Here, they can take magic from humans." He bites his lip. "Through sex."

Oh god, too much detail. Don't say that word in such a low tone with a look like that. Joss's closeness messes with my head, a desire to touch him the way I do when I'm close to Heath. I'm awkward around new people, especially guys, but with these three, it's as if I'm with family. Well, not family, because the way my body's lighting up around Joss isn't familial.

"They crossed over what?"

"Through portals connected to our world."

This is too much crazy talk for me. I sink onto a chair again, and Joss sits opposite me. "I'm lost. In more ways than one."

Joss rubs my arm, as if he needs to place a hand on me to stay connected the way I unknowingly want to. "There are portals in this world to other realms, which need to be kept sealed. Some of these realms are decaying, and when the portals were still open, those whose populations were dying out came through. Vampires, fae, shifters... demons.

Every race that's managed to establish themselves here has something available from humans to replace what they lost. Fae, sexual energy to fuel their magic. Vampires, blood. Shifters, mates."

"And demons?"

"The world." Heath's voice comes from the kitchen doorway, and I turn. He looks between us. "I thought we were going to talk about this together?"

"She's impatient."

"How do you know all this?" I ask.

"Ah, go and find Ewan will you? Haul his lazy ass out of bed." Heath inclines his head to the stairs behind him.

Joss glares at him. "You're closer."

His childish response would amuse me apart from the growl to his voice. Three men in a house together? Their friendship, however tight, will always be threatened by one wanting to be the top dog.

Or four. Where's the other guy, Xander, they mentioned?

In response, Heath drags a chair and sits at the table, back to Joss. "Did you sleep okay?"

"I'm sure she did. My bed's very comfortable," says Joss and winks at me.

Thank god, I'm not a blusher. "Kind of. Well, not really."

"Oh really?" Joss pokes his tongue into his cheek and raises both brows. Okay, I am a blusher right now because I swear he knows what I imagined.

His broad figure leaves the room.

"Your flat's intact, by the way," Heath says. "I headed back after you went to sleep last night. The fire fizzled out, probably when I killed your attackers."

I shudder. "And the bodies?"

"Also fizzled out."

Is he serious? "And this man was a fae?"

"Yeah. We've been watching your flat because we expected this to happen."

I stare. "So you are stalking me! That wasn't a coincidence two nights ago."

"Not stalking you but the people following you. Haven't you been aware?"

I chew my lip. "I'm paranoid people are following me all the time, in reality and online. Considering my extracurricular activities, it comes with the territory."

"Yeah, well that's not paranoia. Only in the last few days have we been sure you're Verity. Or the one we're looking for, anyway."

I run my fingers down my cheek and stare back into his green eyes. Again, I want to reach out and touch him, to hold onto a safety I can't explain. I expected a desire to run from the house as soon as daylight hit but I feel safe with these three men, which makes no sense.

"Verity. Because everybody's looking for the truth, huh?" I give a weak smile.

"I heard Joss explain you were Truth."

"Yes, and Joss said he's a kind of empath too. Two days ago, I would also've said he was slightly unhinged for believing in demons, but now... I think he's sane."

"I'm glad to hear that, Verity."

"Vee. Please can you all stop calling me Verity."

"Yeah, *Death*." Joss reappears and plonks himself back onto a chair next to his friend. "You should understand since *you* don't like your real name either."

"I knew a girl at school who said her surname was De'ath. We joked she's a vampire. Is that why you call yourself Heath?”

Heath scowls and picks at the table. "No. Joss is being awkward."

"There's no getting away from it, Death."

"You want me to tell her who you are?" he retorts.

"Go ahead."

Heath shakes his head. "You're a douche sometimes."

A dishevelled Ewan appears in the doorway, shirtless, sweatpants resting low on his hips. This guy's toned to the point that if I saw him in a magazine, I'd swear he's photoshopped. The ink across his chest and on his arms merges into a canvas I'd love to explore. Bedhead, sexy dark hair, longer than the other guys, is mussed above his bleary eyes.

The guys faces are sculpted the same; do their bodies match too? I'd lay bets they do.

As soon as he looks in my direction, I snap my gaze away. Three men and I'm constantly perving on them all? Really, not good.

"I was up all night coding, can't this wait?" he moans. "I had to finish up before the Order jumped one step ahead."

"And?" asks Heath.

"Their email server is fucked." He turns a rare smile in my direction, eyes filled with a genuine friendliness. "No 'turning it off and back on again.'"

I return his smile. "You work in IT support too?"

"Not really. I work in screwing up everybody else's IT." He flicks long fingers at Heath. "He's Death so his skills are self-explanatory. I'm good at spreading viruses." I look blankly as he gestures at himself. "Pestilence?"

"Ewan...," warns Heath.

"Oh come on. She believes everything else, and it's pretty damn important she knows." He folds his arm across his impressive chest. "We're the Four Horsemen."

"A team of hackers spreading viruses?" I ask. "Is that why you know me? Through the blog and community?"

"No. Actual Four Horsemen," replies Ewan. "Though probably not the version you've heard of."

"I bloody hope not. I'm twenty-one and not keen on an apocalypse just yet!"

Joss chuckles. "You're really not what we expected."

"So you're Famine and he's Pestilence?" I ask semisarcastically. Ewan nods. "And your missing mate... War?"

"Yup."

"So you're a mass murderer?" I ask Heath. Surely this smooth looking guy can't spend time with blood on his hands.

"Only if you count nonhumans. I'm not the only one. They do too." He points at Joss and Ewan. "I just have more control over my victim's afterlife than these guys do."

"Hmm. So I guess your friend War is out hunting *victims*?"

"Well, Xander's more of a strategist, but when he's away this long, it's likely strategising and negotiation have failed, and conflict is the game."

I hold a hand up. "Stop there. Demons, yes. Fae, okay, but Biblical figures? Nope. I told you I don't believe in that crap. How bloody ridiculous, you—"

"I'll drop the last one on you, should I?" interrupts Ewan.

Heath stands and growls, "Ewan. No."

"You're the Fifth," says Ewan.

And grins.

8

VERITY

The room sways and I place my mug on the table before I drop it. "Excuse me? Fifth what?"

"The fifth Horseman. Or 'Horseperson' if you prefer." Ewan's smile snakes further across his face.

Heath steps forward and pushes him in the chest. "Stop screwing with her head, asshole."

Ewan grabs his arm and pushes him to one side. "Why? Why protect her after all this time? We fucking need Verity."

"Not now, Ewan," he says in a low voice. I whip my head from man to man, attempting to keep up with who's telling the truth.

"I'm a harbinger of the apocalypse?" I ask with a side of snark. "Sure."

"A hacker," puts in Joss with a warning look at Ewan.

"He's messing with you. Your skills. You can help us. We're hackers, on the same mission as you to expose people."

I close my eyes and soak in the energies around me, detecting not just their tension, but who's telling me the truth.

"Oh for fuck's sake," says Ewan. "I am not spending the best part of three years looking for our missing part to dance around and ease her into the truth. She's the Fifth and that's it. End of story."

"That's ridiculous. Don't you think I'd know if I was some... whatever you are and not human?" I reply.

"You're human. Unique, but human."

"Bullshit!" I stand and slam my chair backwards. "I've put up with enough of this. I want to leave now. Take me home."

"Vee, no, listen," says Heath.

I need air, not claustrophobia. Huge, lungfuls of fresh air. Stumbling from the room, I make my way back along the slate-tiled hallway to the dark wood front door. Pulling the black metal handle down, I pray the guys haven't locked me in. When the handle moves, stiffly, I throw all my strength into getting out of the house.

The uneven ground around the house is muddy following recent rain, and my shoes squelch as I run across the makeshift driveway towards the lane leading towards the road. But I have no idea where I am? My hair blows behind me as I keep going, my tight chest constricting further as I go. *Run. Leave. Find road. Flag down car.* The escape process runs through my head. I know the surrounding villages around the town, I'm sure I can locate where I am.

Damn the bloody fae for setting fire to my phone.

Fae. Bile rises again and I halt, leaning over and sliding my hands down my knees and tears build. *Please make this stop.* The wind bites my arms through the thin material, cooling the perspiration away from my body. News that vampires and demons are real, that supernatural creatures attacked me, okay, I can accept as the evidence is there. But Horsemen? Me involved in all this? No. Can't be true.

"Vee!" A voice travels through the wind towards me, carrying passed my ears and into the silent space around.

The gate to the road is a few hundred metres away, the house equally as far from where I stand. I spin around in case all three guys are chasing me, but Heath's the one who's approaching. My instinct to run drops away the closer he moves to me, as if something inside tugs me towards him.

"Vee, please stop." He pauses, far enough away to not threaten me. "Please don't leave."

"What's happening?" I say and finally the tears I've held back for hours spill. Pissed off, I scrub a cheek with my sleeve. "Yesterday you asked me out for a drink like we were an ordinary guy and girl, and now I'm wrapped up in something as weird as things I investigate."

"I'm sorry. I wanted to get to know you first so we had some trust. Ease you into the idea."

"Let me guess, the others didn't agree."

"There wasn't any mutual agreement, no." He smiles. "Besides, I liked I had the chance to get to know you better. Made up for taking that shitty job that I had a chance to be around you first."

Heath rubs his mouth, and I watch the action, absentmindedly wondering what his mouth feels like, what would've happened if I kissed him last night.

Last night when the world was different. Recent events slam into my reality again and I heave in a breath, more tears escaping my eyes.

"Oh hell, Vee." Heath takes my hands, and circles them with his strong fingers, holding tight.

We've touched before, fingers brushing, and when he held my hand to help me last night, I never noticed the extent of the effect. This time it's clear. Something more powerful than the attraction I have to him pulses through my blood, sharpening my senses and wiping away the weakness that'd set in with my fear. We look back at each other, transfixed, as I grip him in return.

An energy hums between us, spiralling in the air around, and as we continue to look at each other, this pulls us closer. "Is Ewan telling the truth?" I whisper. "Am I part of... you all?"

"You know he is, Verity," he whispers.

"He can't be. I'm ordinary. Human."

The surging energy builds despite my words, and he pulls me closer. "Yes, but no. You're part of this. Of us. We need you." His chest brushes mine, the thick cotton against my thin shirt, but I feel him as if we were naked, my body firing with a different energy. "Please stay."

I can't let go. Heath doesn't let go. His eyes drop to my mouth, and he grazes his teeth over his bottom lip. My breath catches in my throat.

"Xander was right. He knew when the Fifth arrived, things would become complicated." Heath drops my hand and reaches out to touch my cheek. "He also warned us why the Fifth isn't a man. And that's going to be the biggest complication of all."

I moisten my dry lips, as he shifts and holds his a whisper away from mine. They could be touching, the invisible gap charged with what we both know is inevitable. Heath doesn't need to say anymore as his mouth closes over mine. My body jerks as the energy between us grows, blinding me to everything but the places our bodies touch. Our chaste touch drops as I dig my hands into his hair, and he holds my head, as our mouths move against each other in the unleashed passion of two lovers parted by years and miles.

White light flashes across my mind and images stream through my head. Faces. People. Places. One after another, and I'm unable to grasp anything but glimpses until I see a vision of myself. *I'm on the floor in my flat, ashen white with scratches on my neck, looking back in fear.* A surge of emotions accompanies the image: concern and then anger. As the image of myself continues to look back, a new feeling surges.

Desire to protect. To touch. To hold and not let go.

Heath's memories.

He moves to hold me closer, hands in the small of my back, and my nipples harden as if our skin was touching, and his grip tightens.

I'm not the type of girl who tears clothes off and drags a guy to bed, but it's a bloody good job we're outside in the cold and that any clothing removal would cool the passionate heat. Heath's the epitome of a guy I'd lust over, but this reaction goes beyond purely physical. A different unity exists here, and what I saw seals my belief that I'm part of Heath. Of them.

I pull my mouth away with a gasp, lips swollen, and touch his face. Heath nods and touches my lips, as if aware what I saw when we kissed.

"Well you didn't waste much time, did you?"

I attempt to move away at the sound of the voice, my fingers pulling Heath's as I turn my head to Joss. Joss frowns, hands deep in jacket pockets as he looks at how close Heath and I are.

Heath's grip remains on me. "Vee needs to understand how connected she is."

Joss cocks a brow. "Hmm. Very connected to you, by the looks."

"I told her the connection's to all of us."

"And then what? Kissed her?" Joss scratches his cheek with a thumbnail, then gestures at us. His amused tone switches to warning. "Don't you think this will be complicated enough to begin with, without one of us behaving like this?"

I succeed in detaching myself from Heath and stare at the ground. Is Joss jealous? The heat from our kiss dissipates, apart from my burning cheeks from Joss's arrival.

"I should go," says Heath and tips my chin with two fingers. "Sorry, Vee."

I fight against saying “I'm not,” unashamed, but the tension surrounding prevents me. Heath's footsteps crunch across the gravel, and I look up to see him muttering something in Joss's ear. Joss's steady gaze reaches mine again, and he nods at Heath's words.

As Heath walks away, the energy between us fades, but my desire for him doesn't. Joss runs a hand through his hair and grips the front as he looks back at me.

"I told you, you were too cute. Come on, trouble." Joss winks at me and smiles, but behind the smile, there's something more.

I hesitate, but the decision was made the moment my lips touched Heath's and I saw myself through his eyes. If I'm one fifth of whatever this is, and the other three have the same effect on me, the mysterious Xander's right. Our lives are about to become complicated. Especially mine.

9

Joss

Verity walks back to the house with me, and I fight against striding ahead of her to tell Heath exactly what I think about his actions. Annoyance and jealousy vie for control. I knew Verity would arrive soon; we all did, and I'd already guessed the reaction we'll have, but the guys also agreed not to act on the desire bound to come with meeting her.

Problem: Verity's a part of me in the same way Heath and the other guys are. We're bonded by our creation, the essence inside each of us necessary to hold together five powerful beings and the natural conflict that will arise from the situation. Seriously, without this overarching need to keep each other safe, and to interact and exist in a shared responsibility, I would've walked away by now, duty or no fucking duty.

The four of us also fight like siblings, even though only Heath and Xander are. Still, we're brothers forced to live with each other in our claustrophobic, pressured lives, which often ends in conflict and Xander walking away. His volatile personality doesn't suit any attempt at harmony, but what would anybody expect of War?

We weren't aware Verity existed until three years ago. We've been here ten years, or the current version of the Four have been. Each Horsemen "batch"—because that's how I feel best describes us sometimes—fails, and more filth cross through the portals the Horsemen fail to keep closed. This time, the Fifth is a new addition, something to hold us together. The idea only fully made sense to me when Xander revealed the Fifth was a girl. We'll strive harder to keep her alive. To keep the Truth alive.

The Four are pursued, a lot, and we often find ourselves in situations tricky to escape, but immortality helps with that. Plus, Death on our team can find a permanent solution to those hell-bent on eradicating the Four.

Some supernatural races cooperate with us, especially the fae who don't have anywhere to return to and need to remain here if their population is to survive. Well, they could return to the frozen wasteland their realm became, but they refuse to speak about why they won't, or what happened to force the population to leave.

If anything, the fae's interests lie in helping us keep the portals closed and the human world alive. They've no desire to mix themselves with the demons either. If the demons and Lucifer achieve their desire to eradicate

God's creations and take the world for themselves, there's no knowing how they'll treat the fae. We allow the fae to remain untouched, if they keep their population under control, their peoples' numbers *and* actions.

The Four of us are no longer sure that control's happening. Fae locating and attempting to take Verity before we found and approached her doesn't bode well for our shaky alliance. Especially considering Heath killed the fae guy.

Was he rogue? Or a true example of the fae attitude to our relationship now the demons' tendrils spread further through every society?

I blow air into my cheeks as I walk back into the building. The whole time she's spent inside the house, Verity's face has been pale and eyes filled with trepidation. Now there's colour to her cheeks, put there by Heath. Irritation surges again. As the first to see her weeks ago, Heath warned us that Xander was right and the effect on us won't be easy to keep a handle on. I thought Heath meant when we were close to her, but not a head-splitting need to touch her from standing in the same bloody room.

Is Vee aware what happened between her and Heath outside is more than kissing the cute guy she met at work? If that was an attempt to tell herself she's capable of normality, she's turned in the wrong direction.

Girls we meet on our rare nights off "work" attempt to get up close and personal with Heath within a few hours; that's nothing new, but he shouldn't have been so accommodating to Vee.

The issue here I don't want to admit, even though the voice nags, is I wish I'd been in his place. Seeing them stabbed anger into my mind and disappointment into my stomach, unwarranted and a huge surprise.

The douche just made things awkward for all of us.

Verity meets my eyes, the way she has many times since we met, but this time she looks away and focuses on her hands instead. Disappointment she's breaking the building understanding that we're attracted to each other, and this could mean more, pushes in and I glare at Heath instead.

At least he isn't standing next to her, Verity's big protector who rescues her from demons. Yeah, well, when we've taught Vee how powerful she is, she won't need his bullshit knight-in-shining-armour act.

Heath notices my look and inclines his head to Ewan, with a small shake. I'm half-tempted to tell Ewan what Heath did, but if Vee sees us in full-blown conflict mode, she'll definitely run for the hills.

Still shirtless, Ewan's laptop-free for once and scouting the kitchen for food. Ewan's denied Vee had any major effect on him, but come on, the guy must know walking around seminaked in front of a girl fated to be attracted to him sends her signals.

But I guess Ewan's a slob and has sworn off spending time alone with her; maybe I'm overthinking this, and one of us at least has his head screwed on around Vee.

Vee sits at the table again, arms crossed in the defensive way she has most of the time she's around us. She runs her tongue along her lips, stirring my desire to do the same, and I look away.

"Four Horsemen?" she asks in a low voice. "Is this why a fae invaded my home last night?"

"Yes."

"And I've always had this"—she makes inverted commas with her fingers—"uniqueness."

"Yes. We've only recently discovered you exist, and we've spent the last few months looking for and choosing the right time to approach you," says Heath.

Vee nods, as if the words have added believability coming from his mouth out of the three of us.

"We were hoping to gradually get to know you rather than this mindfuck as you call it," I put in. "Sorry."

She narrows her eyes at Heath. "Is this why I didn't hurt you with my car?"

"Yeah, you can't kill Death." One corner of his mouth lifts up in a smile. "Or any of us. No human can."

"But I can be killed? Nice. I'm in your gang and not equal."

"No, you can't be killed," replies Ewan.

Her mouth parts in surprise. "What? Because I'm Truth. Ha. People kill the truth all the time."

"Not really," says Heath with a smile. "The Truth always survives. We all do, none of us can be beaten."

"At least you're not Famine," I put in. "I spend half my life accidentally soaking up and experiencing the emotions of others, which can leave them hungering for basic human needs. Food. Warmth. Comfort. Love." Vee's troubled look pushes me to explain myself, which I hate. "Not deliberately. I have control and can save my *talent* for those who deserve to be starved of those things."

"He's a good cook though," pipes up Heath.

"Screw you."

"And what do you do?" she asks Heath.

"I'm usually out helping my brother, but sometimes he works without me," he says evasively.

"Or sometimes they hang around here fighting," Ewan replies.

"Seems you all like to do that," Vee says. "Are you all related?”

"No but we may as well be," mutters Ewan.

I zone out and leave the talking to Heath and Ewan, although most talking comes from Heath. Don't they understand that all the time spent talking to Vee equals time lost to track down who's behind the attack on her? Ewan may've warded the property, but Vee has a job and life, which I doubt she'll give up readily to fight alongside us. Whether she'll have the choice or not remains to be seen, but Vee definitely won't be able to continue her human existence indefinitely.

I catch up with Heath as he sorts through his weapons in the lounge room, removing each knife from its sheath and inspecting the blade. When he hears my footsteps, Heath slams the long black case closed and spins around.

He purses his lips at me. "Oh. Thought you might be Verity. She isn't a fan of weapons."

"She prefers to be called Vee."

Heath shoves thick dark hair from his brow and studies me. "Don't walk in here and start lecturing me."

"Start? What the hell was that? You and her?"

His eyes widen, and he walks to the door, closing it quietly. "It wasn't supposed to happen."

"Damn straight, Heath."

"I thought Vee was leaving, looked bloody terrified,

Joss." He scrunches his face as he pauses. "And she *cried*, for fucks sake. I held her hands, tried to let Vee know we were here for her and wouldn't hurt her and..."

"And what?"

"Fucking boom." He makes exploding motions with his fingers. "Her energy slammed into my chest. I could hardly breathe for a moment, and then suddenly I was kissing her and she was kissing me, and it was so bloody intense."

"Which is exactly why we were told to keep hands off her! No. Touching. The. Fifth."

"Yeah, well I'd touched Vee a few times helping out in the last day or so and nothing happened. I thought Xander had exaggerated and we'd be okay."

I dig hands into my pockets. "You know this isn't because she wants *you,* right? Could be any of us. All of us."

Heath shrugs. "Yeah, whatever. I think we sparked before she knew who I was."

"No, listen. It's unfair. She feels what you do, but for all of us, if we touch. The four of us guys? Yeah, we can notice each other's power and unite to strengthen that, but she has the guy-girl thing to deal with on top of the bond."

"You heard from Xander?" he asks.

I narrow my eyes at his subject change. "No. I've only spoken to his voicemail."

"There's something bloody strange going on." Heath turns back and reopens the black case, then runs a finger along above the knives before selecting the same one he took yesterday. Short, carved-ivory handle. Iron blade. "You know what I think?"

I shake my head at him as he turns. "Someone's trying to distract us."

"Obviously, otherwise they wouldn't have got to Vee before us."

"No, trying to distract us from investigating Mr Big's latest venture."

Mr Big, our unoriginal nickname for the head honcho demon, Lucifer's guy on the ground. AKA Evil bastard. His web extends around the world, wrapped around people and organisations I'm sure we only know the half of it. Every time we track him down, he's moved on, leaving footprints in trails of blood behind. Sometimes literally.

"Big's attempting to hook up with the Nightwalkers again."

"Huh? Nobody can negotiate with that vamp clan. They don't have the brains to join in scheming."

Heath pulls a derisive face. "Did you think perhaps that's the reason he chose them? They're brutal. Handy allies who're easily influenced."

"Man, this is all getting too hard."

Heath gestures at the door with his knife. "We have the Fifth now. We're stronger."

In some ways, but what about divisions the Fifth causes already?

Ten minutes later, I watch through the kitchen window as Vee walks to Heath's SUV with him. Heath's distance from her is a lot bloody better than the last time I saw them together.

I just hope he listened.

10

VERITY

Singe marks cover my bedroom carpet, and the light fittings melted. A burnt electrical smell hangs in the air. The black marks on the floor are damp from somebody extinguishing the fire, but apart from that. my room's unscathed. Ha ha. How am I supposed to explain this one to my landlord?

When I arrived with Heath, my flat appeared the same as yesterday from the outside, although the prospect of heading inside didn't appeal. My memories of supernatural creatures attempting to abduct and/or strangle me and mysterious fires in the house didn't encourage me back.

Heath reassures me he and Joss checked the place out last night and I'm safe to go inside, but I hung back and followed him cautiously into the flat.

Now, I stand in the bedroom doorway and chew a nail, looking between the mess in the room and in my flat. If Heath hadn't been with me, I doubt I would've set foot in here. The moment I did, I pictured myself pinned against the wall by the demon, terrified I'd be strangled, burned alive, or both.

"I don't think you should stay here," says Heath, echoing my thoughts.

I look over my shoulder where he stands in the open doorway watching the stairs. His uncertainty whether we were followed is enough to prompt my resounding agreement, but I'm pissed off that someone's forcing me from my home.

The drive back to my place from the guys' house was filled with the same heavy silence as yesterday. Last time, I sat beside Heath shaking and in shock. This time, the unspoken kiss filled the humming air between us.

I'm trying to get my head around the fact I'm a... whatever a Horseman is, and all I can focus on is my encounter with Heath.

One he's avoiding by saying the bare minimum to me today and completely avoiding the topic, as if the intense kiss never happened.

I heard raised voices between Joss and Heath before we left, and I want to ask why, but the evidence is in front of me. Heath crossed a line, and he's backed away.

"I was thinking." Heath watches as I tuck my laptop into the rucksack filled with my clothes and essentials. "Do you still have the meeting arranged with the guy from your online group? I'm wondering if he has anything to do with this."

"To be honest, that's the furthest thing from my mind right now."

The tension grows, but for the first time he holds my gaze long enough for me to see a confusion to match mine. "Everything is complicated, Vee."

"You're telling me," I say with a small laugh.

I will him to walk over and put his arms around me, to tell me everything will be okay, but do I really want him to lie? No.

"I think you should. One of us will go with you, just in case...." Heath trails off.

Just in case someone else tries to drag me off god knows where?

"Okay. We arranged to meet next week."

"Where?"

"In town at one of the cafes, Coffee Spot. Public."

Heath nods slowly. "I'll talk to the guys and see if they agree."

Nothing more is said as I follow him from the flat with my gear in a rucksack. As the damage is less than I expected, I could stay if I put up with the burnt smell, but my unease inside the place sends me home with Death.

On the way back to the boys' place, I steal a glance at him as he drives. He's dressed in a plaid shirt beneath his army green jacket, large hands sliding across the wheel. Anytime I'm in close proximity to any of these guys, my chest flutters. Is that because of this connection? Exactly what is my connection?

I sigh and stare out the window, watching the ploughed fields rush by. I am not avoiding this anymore. "So, you're Death, are you?"

"Heath."

"But also the Horseman Death?" He doesn't reply, and I grit my teeth. "And I'm Truth?"

"Fancy names for a shit role, that's all. Like Joss said last night, stories passed down by generations tend to become embellished." He flicks the indicator switch as we take a turn into the final street before his place. "We're here to stop the apocalypse, not start it."

"I know, you said, but—"

He shoots me a tired look. "I don't like talking to you about this without the other guys around, sorry."

I shuffle down in my seat, fighting a pout. Fine.

Back at the house, I'm given Joss's room to dump my bag in. I'm given more information I don't want to hear when I protest I'm taking up his space.

"It doesn't matter. We're moving on soon," says Ewan. "Joss can crash in my room for a few days."

"Moving on where?" I ask.

"North."

"Well that narrows the location down," I mutter.

Joss, whose flirting behaviour dropped as quickly as Heath's gives me one of his warm smiles, as if he knows this helps settle my nerves.

"One of the portals is in the area we're headed, and there's been more activity around there. The vampire population in the area are pretty much under control, but there've been a few unwanted deaths so we need to check what's happening," says Joss.

"Unwanted deaths? So what constitutes a wanted death?" I ask laying on the sarcasm.

"Dead demons," says Heath in a low voice.

"Oh. Okay. Well, I asked for that one."

"We think that might be where Xander is," puts in

Heath. "We were going to move on as soon as we found you, but I spoke to Joss and Ewan. We want to know who this guy is that's contacted you."

"If he is a guy," replies Ewan.

Whoa. I sit in silence and watch the conversation and dynamic around me. They discuss plans, only half-involving me, and I attempt to switch off from their insanity. Each time I pull back from what's happening in front of me, reality swirls around my head and disappears down a huge hole. I always suspected the world's different than the one presented to the masses, but never that mine was this.

11

VERITY

Ewan kicks back, watching TV with a beer in his hand while Joss and Heath head out for the evening without any explanation to me. Killing random inhuman creatures or a trip to the pub again? If Ewan's here, I'm guessing the killing option. I watch him for a moment. Will he continue his semisnarky attitude to me if I sit and talk?

Instead of joining him, I take my laptop into the kitchen and immerse myself back into the world of conspiracy and secrets.

The message boards have been quiet since I last visited, and I've no messages from DoomMan. I fire off a quick one to him and confirm our meeting next week. Most people I communicate with are in Europe and the States, so he either is travelling a long way to see me or is local. He never said. Is DoomMan one from the secretive new group, Red Virus?

I pull on my bottom lip as I click through the latest news uploaded to the site. Due to the recent mind-blowing information about demons and other races, I begin to form new theories how the faceless people control society. This could explain the unexplained deaths and disappearances of key political and business figures too. No wonder whistle-blowers are too scared to step forward, the last two died by suicide.

I work though news reports centred around the North of England and into Scotland but find nothing to suggest why the guys are headed there. This raises more questions. What do these portals look like? How do the guys protect them? Each click, each article, and my confusion grows.

I slump back in my chair and stare at the screen.

"You want a beer?" Ewan stands by the fridge, door open.

I can't hide my surprise at his talking to me. Ordinarily, I'd avoid spending time around a guy with the look and demeanour Ewan has. His imposing look, messy hair, and tattoos, along with his height matching the other guys, overshadow. As with all three, my wariness doesn't extend to my hormones. I definitely need to avoid physical contact with him. Or anybody who lives here.

"Maybe one beer. It might calm my nerves."

He grabs a beer and pops off the top before setting it on the table in front of me. "Don't be nervous, I'm a nice guy really. Research?" He points at the laptop.

"Just trying to keep some of my everyday normality."

Ewan pulls out a chair and sits beside me, resting his

forearms on the table. The tattoos show as his shirtsleeves ride up.

"I guess you can wave normality goodbye. What are you looking at?"

He leans forward to study my laptop screen, and I hold my breath against his scent, at how his arm brushing mine induces the same butterfly-craziness in my stomach.

"Just keeping up with what's happening in the world."

"Right." Ewan shifts in his seat and drinks as he watches me.

"So am I allowed to hunt the bad guys too?" I ask with a laugh.

"Well, they'll be hunting you so I imagine you'd better."

I stop typing, fingers resting on the laptop keys. "You don't hold back do you?"

My heart rate increases as he tugs on his lip with his teeth. "Yeah, I do." He switches to what I presume he thinks is a reassuring smile. "You should be kept up to speed on everything, now you're with us."

"I appreciate that."

Ewan shrugs and points his bottle at the laptop. "I probably cause some of the problems you fix at work."

"Huh. Thanks."

"You know there's at least one demon who works at your place, right?"

"I bet it's Charlotte. She's a real bitch." We share a smile. “I didn’t know, but I guess if Death works there, a demon can too."

"Precisely." He laughs. "You're coping with this better than I thought."

"Do I have any choice?"

"Well, you're coming with us, when we leave."

"Was that a suggestion or a statement?"

"A bit of both. I'm forthright as you probably noticed."

"I did."

Ewan runs a hand across the day's growth on his cheek. "We need your help, Verity. Without you, the other four of us are weaker." He pauses and sets down the bottle. "The other guys think you need easing into the idea, but that's what caused the fae to get to you first. Inaction. You're safer here, and I sense you're okay to be with us?"

I chew my lip and look back at my screen. "Yes, but I'm not sure I trust you totally."

"Understandable and that's another reason I don't agree with keeping things from you."

"What things?"

"I've told you most of it." *Most?* "Hang on." Ewan leaves the room and reappears with his laptop, which he places on the table and sits next to me. "Want to see what I've been working on too?"

"Sure." I shift my chair closer.

Over the next half hour, Ewan takes me through pages of code, some I only half-understand, and in front of my eyes, hacks into MI5 emails. The encryption takes a few minutes for Ewan's program to pull apart, and he brings us more beers as we watch his virus spread.

"Wow. I know people who've spent years trying to get to this level of hacking."

He grins. "Pestilence, remember?"

I stiffen. "I try not to."

"Don't worry, I'm not infectious unless I want to be, and then I'm *really* infectious."

"Do I want to know?" I ask.

"I kill, but not people," he says in a flat voice. "And I stick to this damage usually."

"Good to hear. I pick up viruses really easily."

Ewan chuckles. "You pick up viruses? So, you'd pick up Pestilence?"

I meet his eyes, hoping that he's teasing, but his guarded nature doesn't give me any clues. The silence hovers, as we attempt to read each other, and I hope he fails too.

"How're your finances?" he asks, eventually.

"Not great."

Ewan nods and opens another window on his screen. "You need a new ID if you're joining the gang. May as well give you a healthy bank balance too. Any names you prefer?"

"Names?"

I blink at how rapidly he runs through a set of sites, creating a new identity and medical records, dragging my picture from one to another. He sits back. "There you go. You're now also called Hope Springs."

"You can't do that!"

"Just did."

"You seriously chose to give me that name?"

Ewan gives me a sly smile and hovers his fingertips above the keys. "I can change it if you want."

"And you steal?"

"From selective accounts of those who have too much. We don't work unless we have to. You should've seen the sulking when Heath drew the short straw and had to take the job at your place."

I smile. "I only saw him from a distance, and he always looked like he was perfecting the hot, brooding image. He was just a grumpy ass, huh?"

"Hot and brooding Heath? Ha. Yeah, girls fall for our friend Death a lot. Beer?"

"Sure." I swallow down the rising jealousy, but he hasn't commented on the kiss, so how could it mean anything? His response irritates me, but it really isn't the hardest thing I'm dealing with right now. Plus, I'm fighting attraction to his friends so it would be hypocritical of me to be too pissed off.

Maybe they should bottle and sell whatever testosterone they have because it must be bloody strong stuff.

Ewan relaxes around me as we chat about computers, and the sites he visits in his search for unusual events, although his are for different reasons to me. He shows me around the spreadsheets and graphs cataloguing his research. Strange for their activities, but suit his analytical attitude.

"Where exactly are Heath and Joss?" I ask.

"Mopping up. Rogue shifter."

Vampires. Shifters. "Rogue? Killing people?"

"Werewolf. He's only killing other dogs now, but he's bound to move on."

"To people?" I ask in horror. "How do you allow that?"

"The shifters police themselves, but some reach adulthood and lose the ability to control their nature. Then they turn rogue, and we are called in to clean up."

"You kill them?"

"Yeah. The packs don't care. They don't want their society threatened. They live amongst us mostly peacefully. Same as the vampires."

"Vampires? Peaceful?”

"Relatively speaking." He grins. "They have donors and very strict rules. If any vampire steps out of line, the leaders of the Houses will rip their heads off. Literally."

"Whoa." I blink. "You know, Ewan, every time I feel I'm getting a handle on this, you land more weirdness on me.

"The problem is the demons influence is growing and the peace amongst the societies fading."

I rub my temples before picking up my drink and draining the bottle. "Sounds like you have your work cut out."

"We can decimate them in minutes if they step out of line, but the numbers who do are growing."

I watch him, more animated as the alcohol subdues whatever guards him against me. Although the others don't lie to me, they hold back the truth, and I appreciate this. Do they think I can't deal with everything?

"I think I'd rather help you with the research side rather than the hunting," I admit.

Ewan laughs. "I do both. The other guys aren't clever enough to do this part."

"I bet they wouldn't like to hear you say that."

"Ah. They 'do' rather than think. Especially Heath and Xander. Instinct versus intellect." He smirks. "But don't tell them I said that. Beer?"

I pick at the label on my bottle debating whether to ask for another or head to bed. "I'm tired."

Ewan's eyes widen as he stands. "No problem. I have a show I'm watching. I'll leave you alone."

"No. I don't mean I want you to leave me alone. I'm genuinely tired." I stand too.

Ewan drags a hand through his hair and takes a deep breath before releasing it and shaking his head. "Can I ask, and tell, you one more thing?"

Hairs on my neck stand to alert. "About you four or me?"

"Both. About our bond to each other as Horsemen. It's unbreakable. We can't walk away from this even if we wanted to. As guys, that makes us brothers in a way, but I don't think that brotherly nature will apply to you."

"Are you telling me I won't really be allowed to get close to you?"

He quirks a brow and steps closer. "What happens when you do get close to us?"

The energy pulls again, blotting my thoughts and switching all my focus to the man in front of me. My awareness magnifies as the same energy coils around and pulls me into imagining how soft his lips are, how I could run my fingers along the taut abs I saw this morning.

Definitely not sisterly on my part. Does he know what happened with Heath?

"I feel the bond when I get close," I say, eyes remaining on his. "That's all."

"But not just to me, right? To all of us? I don't think it will be possible for us to keep you at a distance without concentrating really hard." He lifts a hand and tucks a strand of hair behind my ear, the featherlight sensation of his finger against the skin sparking across my scalp. "So if I keep my distance, don't presume that I'm a rude bastard, but just that I don't want this"—he gestures between us—"fucking things up."

Mouth dry, I nod.

"I worry you could weaken the bond. We may be immortal, but parts of us are very human." My power of speech remains absent at his undertones. "What I'm saying is, you need to be part of all of us or none of us, Vee, and I'd prefer the 'none' option. Emotions will become involved, and things could become messy."

I step backwards, away from the conversation. Do I thank him for his forthright words even though they scare me? Ewan's exact meaning isn't hard to grasp. What happened with Heath. How Joss reacted. My desire to be around them that's prevented me running. This is all part of something bigger.

Why the hell did whoever created this make the Fifth a woman?

12

VERITY

The three guys are spread around the house when I wake the next morning. Ewan's still in bed, Heath's in the kitchen, and Joss is in the lounge, bare feet on the table and paperback in hand. I incline my head to read the cover on the way passed but don't recognise the title.

"Morning, Vee." He waves a hand without looking up.

"Hey."

"Are you enjoying your time in my bed?"

Joss still doesn't look at me, but I don't miss his fighting a smile.

"I've had more interesting times in a man's bed," I reply. "Not so much in yours."

His head snaps up from the book, and I arch a brow. He'll soon learn that a more relaxed Vee will mean less silence against his banter. "Well, we can fix that. Just say the word."

I leave him with a smile and a question mark over whether I'm interested. Then walk straight into Heath, who has a weird selection of items on the kitchen table in front of him. One I recognise as the knife he used on the demon the other night.

"Are we headed for a fun day out?" I ask, indicating his jacket slung across the back of the chair.

"We're headed into town to see Portia, our local fae queen."

I blink. "Local fae queen? How many are there?"

"A few. We need to explain ourselves to this one, right, Heath?" Joss walks in and drops the paperback on the table. "You got more holy water for me?"

Heath tosses him a small bottle from the table; one I'd thought was alcohol and been confused why Heath needed to drink on the job.

"Has Xander called?" asks Joss.

Joss shakes his head.

"For fuck's sake. I'm beginning to worry now. What exactly caused your bust up this time?"

“I disagreed with him on strategy. Usual shit. I told you."

Joss shakes his head.

“Is he okay?” I ask.

"He can look after himself,” says Heath with a laugh.

"With water and a knife, I suppose?" I ask.

"Take one." Heath gestures at the table.

"What?"

"A knife, Vee."

I cross my arms. "Really? Your idea of diplomacy is

marching into an audience with a queen carrying a knife?"

"Audience?" Joss laughs. "He's right, though. Take one."

I stare down at the selection on the table. The only knives I usually touch are when I'm chopping vegetables. "I might leave the killing to you."

"Just for self-defence, Vee."

The new estate in the village, close to my town, houses the wealthier end of our population. West Fordham and outlying villages are popular with commuters; people endure long journey times to London in order to afford bigger and better houses than if they chose to live in the city. Few of the town's original residents live in the architecturally designed and perfectly planned estate. Parks intersperse the large two-storey houses, and every detached home boasts immaculate gardens and at least two expensive cars in driveways.

Nobody I know lives here; most are families originally from elsewhere and tend to keep themselves away from the local population.

I thought we'd taken a wrong turn when we pulled into the estate. This isn't where I'd expect a fae queen to reside.

I stare at the large brick residence with Tudor-style windows as Heath parks beside the Range Rover in the driveway. Pink and white roses border the lawn and the windows shine, pathways free from dirt and leaves.

"A queen lives here?"

"Where did you expect her to live?" asks Ewan, opening his door and jumping down from the seat beside me, in the rear of Heath's SUV. "In the middle of the woods? The bottom of your garden?"

Yes. "No."

My car door opens and Heath stands there. "When I said the supernatural live amongst us, I meant literally. Hiding in plain sight, the easiest way to stay disguised."

"Makes sense, I guess."

"I hope she's in a good mood," replies Joss as we head towards the front porch.

"I suspect not," says Heath, "so be respectful."

"Always."

If the fae's suburban house choice was a surprise, the queen herself is a total shock. In my imagination, the fae queen not only lives in a secret palace, glamoured by magic so the human world couldn't see, but also glides around in a silk gown with subjects following and bowing to her every whim.

The woman who answers the door wears black and pink yoga pants with a matching jacket, expensive sneakers, and white blonde hair scraped back into a severe ponytail. Her eye make-up and lipstick accentuate her flawless pale skin as she studies us with a disdainful curve to her mouth.

"Hello, Pony Boys."

Ewan mutters something under his breath.

The woman sweeps a calculating gaze the length of me, then tips her chin. "I'm Portia."

"Hi." I cringe. Hi?

The woman ushers us inside.

"Come."

Of everything bizarre in the situation, the fae's eyes strike me the most. They're the same violet colour as the man Heath killed.

Neatness in this house borders on OCD. By the door, shoes are arranged on a rack in size order, as are the coats, and the colours all complement each other. Mirrors line the hallway, interspersed with studio-quality family photos. The stunning parents, their beautiful children, and obligatory cute baby pictures. Two girls, one a teenager and the other much younger.

We head passed an open doorway, and I catch sight of a teenage girl in the kitchen. She looks up from her phone as we go by. Despite her unusual colouring, the girl's beautiful. White-blonde hair spilling over her shoulders. Her sleeveless My Chemical Romance tee has seen better days, and her black jeans accentuate her long legs and slender figure.

"Sweetheart, please get ready for hockey. We need to leave as soon as I've dealt with business," says Portia.

The teen smiles coyly at one of the guys behind me before pouting at her mother. "But Hunter is coming over this afternoon."

"Really, Elyssia, I've asked you not to invite your friends here without asking me first."

"I didn't think you'd be here," she mutters, and the two glare at each other.

"Tell him you're busy." Portia gestures at Elyssia's phone. A younger girl's voice calls for her mum from somewhere else inside the house. "And please change your sister's clothes. She's covered in mud from playing in the garden and upstairs refusing to change."

I can safely say a teenage fae eye-roll perfectly imitates a human one.

"This way." Portia opens a door leading towards a basement and switches on the light. I follow the guys down carpeted stairs and step into a large room covered in assorted craftwork. The room contains everything from scrapbooking to embroidery, the walls covered in shelves and boxes; framed pictures created by children on the walls.

School mum fae queen who holds meetings with her supernatural associates amongst glue guns and sequins? This world shifts from freaky to unreal as the days pass.

"Are you the Fifth?" Portia asks, studying me more closely this time.

My jeans and hoodie combination make me feel like a hobo in comparison to Portia, even though she's dressed casually too. I'm not wearing a lick of make-up and my ponytailed hair doesn't match her sleekness.

"I'm Verity."

She nods. "Nice to meet you."

"Uh. Likewise."

She gestures to a nearby small sofa close to tall bookshelves and I sit. The guys remain standing, grouped together around her crafting table.

Portia picks up a large pair of scissors and examines them. "Could you explain to me why he"—she points at Heath with the pointed ends—"killed a fae. Big. Fat. No."

Her smooth voice switches to harsh, the tone of somebody used to obedience. *Straight down to business, then.*

"Could you explain why a fae attempted to abduct

Verity and was in the company of a demon?" retorts Heath.

Joss places a hand on his arm. "Heath made a mistake. He understands he should've apprehended the fae instead, but he feared for Vee's safety."

Portia studies me again and wrinkles her nose. "Verity is a Horseman. She could defend herself."

"She doesn't know how," replies Heath. "Not yet."

"Give the girl credit. Her instincts would kick in." She smiles at me. "You have powers that would make any fae proud."

I snap my head around to the guys. Powers? Isn't my self-defence knives?

"That doesn't alter the fact the blue-haired bastard had a demon choking the life from her," snaps Heath.

"Heath!" hisses Joss.

Portia sets down the scissors and turns her face to me. "Blue hair? Did he give a name?" I shake my head.

Silence falls as Portia carefully rearranges items on the table in front of her, long fingers straightening books and tucking items in drawers. I glance at Joss who shrugs. "I'll look into this. Thank you," says Portia, eventually.

Heath steps forward. "Look into it?"

Portia's violet eyes fix on his. "Yes, and if you'd kindly refrain from murdering my kin, that would help us agree to your requests for our aid."

This isn't the reaction they expected, that's clear, but what was?

"Heath kills a fae, who's attempting to abduct our Fifth, and you'll 'look into it'. What the fuck is going on?" says Ewan in a low voice. "Is this something out of your control?"

I recoil as the woman's eyes flash a sudden brighter violet and an energy builds around her. "I will ensure everything is under my control. Do not interfere again."

"So why summon us here?" asks Heath.

"To warn you some may not be as forgiving as me. I am of the opinion that any of my kin who transgress should be dealt with, and I'm happy to do so myself." She pauses. "*Myself.* Not you. There are those in my society who don't trust the Horsemen and will see more sinister reasons behind your actions, Heath. They will use this incident as a reason not to cooperate. You made a very stupid move there."

"Stupid? Listen, we help the fae remain hidden and protected, and in return, you agree to keep your people under control. If you can't manage, then the four of us step in to fix the problem." Heath's muscles stiffen and he makes to step forward towards Portia, but holds himself back.

The building energy in the room shimmers around Portia as her delicate features transform into hard anger. "You need us as much as we need you, boy. Don't forget that small fact."

Joss grips Heath's sleeve. "Heath, calm down. Leave it."

"But if some of you are siding with demons—" Heath's interrupted as his voice chokes into a rasp. I shift on the sofa in alarm as I watch their exchange, and at the fae queen holding a hand out, fingers twisting as she points at his neck.

"Your friend, Death, needs keeping under control," she says, not taking her eyes from him. "Where's War? He can smack some sense into him."

"Xander's missing," replies Joss.

"Oh? So you can accuse me of not controlling my people, while you have no idea where one of yours is or what he's doing?" She sneers. "How do you know he isn't siding with the Order? We're aware you're associated with a demon connected to them."

"How do you know about that?" shoots back Joss.

"Stupid pony boy, we've followed him for a while, and we watch you carefully too. Shouldn't *I* be the one not trusting *you*?"

She steps towards a still speechless Heath and trails long fingers along his cheek and across his lips, her manicured nails catching. "I'm still waiting for your decision on who you choose to seal your unity with *us*. Instead you side with demons." Her mouth twitches, and she moistens her glossed lips as she moves her face closer to Heath's. "Have you decided yet?"

Is she going to kiss him? My heart thumps. This situation becomes weirder by the moment. School-mum fae and death personified together?

"I'm sure your king will love the idea of a *unity*," says Joss with a laugh.

She drops her fingers from Heath and approaches Joss instead. He remains impassive as Portia runs fingers through his hair. "You know I'm not in the habit of limiting myself to one consort. Why should a powerful woman?" She arches a perfectly plucked brow at me and gestures at the three men. "Correct?"

Heat builds in my cheeks at her suggestion that I might follow a similar belief, not wanting to admit to myself that the idea appeals.

"Have you met the delightful Xander yet?" she asks me.

"No. Not yet."

"He's my favourite." She pats Joss on the cheek with her fingertips. "Sorry, beautiful."

Ewan crosses his arms as Portia sets her sights on him. “Don’t bother.”

I bite back a laugh as she pouts, then shakes her head at him.

Never in my life have I seen three men totally silenced by one woman. Are they staying diplomatic, or are genuinely stunned by her behaviour? The guys and Portia are familiar with each other, that's clear. But how familiar?

Portia laughs, the sound chiming around the room. "Oh so serious, boys." She turns to me. "Verity, I do hope you're going to keep them in check now you've found them."

"Me?" I indicate myself and look back at the three men who could take on two of me in a fight and win. "I think they make their own minds up."

She holds up her little finger. "You have more power just in here than the guys—and over them."

"Stop this. How do we sort out this demon problem?" rasps Heath, finding his voice.

"I said I will deal with issues within my community. You deal with yours."

The door handle rattles. "Mummy!"

Portia drops her invisible grip on Heath, who massages his throat and draws in a breath. She shoos the guys out of the way and pulls open the door. "Yes, sweetie?"

A girl, maybe five years old, white blonde hair to match the others and the palest blue eyes I've seen looks up. "Elyssia's being mean to me! She won't let me wear my princess costume!" The girl's dressed in a thin white vest, which reaches half way down her knees.

"Mummy's busy right now, Kailey. Tell Elyssia you can wear what you want." Portia glances at the clock on the wall. "I won't be long."

"And I can't find my princess shoes!"

"Have you looked under your bed?"

"No."

I stare at the ordinary, family conversation taking place in front of me. Are her children fae too?

"This one's half-human," whispers Joss as the pair's conversation continues.

"Can you actually read my mind?" I hiss.

"No, but almost. The look on your face asks the question."

"Elyssia says she wants to be with her boyfriend instead. He just arrived to see her. She told him you're a bitch and won't let—"

I almost choke at the word coming from the little girl's mouth. Portia's lips pull tight, and she lifts Kailey out of the doorway. The girl's eyes fill with tears as her mum sets her on the ground.

"Whoa," mutters Ewan. "Who knew fae had teenage girl problems too?"

Joss's eyes narrow as he watches the door. "No. This is different."

"What's wrong?" asks Heath.

"Follow her." Joss rushes from the room, and I freeze as a scream from upstairs echoes through the house.

Heath's out the door behind Joss in seconds, Ewan

closes and stands in front, ear to the door and holding the handle.

A woman's scream chills my blood, and I grab Kailey's arm as she cries out and attempts to pass Ewan. Ewan rests against the door, knuckles whitening as he holds the handle. His attempt to pull on a calm expression doesn't fool me.

"Is everything okay?" I whisper.

He glances at the girl, then to me. "Well, there's no point in me lying to you, is there?"

No.

"I want, Mummy!" protests Kailey.

"Verity will stay here with you, I'll find out what's happening. Everything will be okay." Ewan's awkwardness around kids shines through, as does his doubt.

"But I want Mummy!" she repeats in a louder voice.

"Can you wait here with her?" asks Ewan. "I'll be back in a few."

"But—" There's no point continuing the sentence as Ewan's through the door in seconds.

All three guys responding to a screaming queen? I'm not familiar with their tactics but this does not bode well. I attempt to calm my nerves and turn to Kailey.

"Should we sit down? Tell me about your favourite princess." I guide her to the sofa. I half-listen as she regales me with tales of Disney princesses. I'm partly amused; does Kailey know she's a real princess? Is she? God, I don't know.

Another scream sounds above. The last one betrayed fear. This one, pain.

The world shifts sideways again.

13

HEATH

I emerge from Portia's strange audience room and into the brightly lit hallway, head snapping from side to side as I attempt to find the source of the screaming. Joss's reaction pounds blood into my limbs, ready to strike. There's something or someone wrong here.

He charges into the nearby lounge room and halts in the doorway. "Shit!"

"What?"

I barge passed him and freeze at the scene in front of me. The room's large with high ceilings, brightly polished marble floor to match the decorative pillars in the centre of the room. A large table, adorned with a vase filled with violets and wildflowers, takes the space close to the glass doors and scenic oil paintings cover the walls.

And Elyssia, the teen who always gives me the eye when we visit, is pinned against the wall by a hulking demon, built like the proverbial and unpleasantly similar to the one who held Verity the other night.

Portia lies on the floor close by, curled in a ball; a second demon stands over her with a long chain wrapped around his broad hand, whip-like, and ready to strike.

Iron.

Holy fuck.

She cowers, aware the damage the chain could cause —not just visible injury but a deeper poison if the metal breaks the skin. The humming presence in the room blocks her magic, as does her daughter held hostage against the wall, life threatened.

A guy stands in the centre of the room, arms outstretched in greeting with a sardonic smile on his face.

I charge towards him, ready to end the situation and the three, shocked and winded as I'm knocked back by a barrier I'm unable to see.

Steadying myself on the wall, I study him. The guy's tall, attractive, dressed in the fashion I've seen around the town amongst kids Elyssia's age and social group. Hair carefully spiked, deep brown eyes. His black jeans and band T-shirt combination match Elyssia's, and he wears thick leather and silver bands around both wrists.

Is this Hunter, Elyssia's boyfriend she mentioned in the kitchen? Or a demon? An uncomfortable feeling prickles. Both.

"How the hell did you find your way into my house?" hisses Portia.

Elyssia cries, gasping against the larger demon's chokehold.

"That's no way to talk about your daughter's lover," he says and tuts.

"Lover?" Portia shrieks. "She's eighteen years old!"

He approaches Elyssia and strokes her long hair. Elyssia spits in his face and he sneers, stepping back and wiping his cheek. "Did you really expect her human nature to control the... shall we say 'passionate' side of her fae?"

"Elyssia would know you were a demon!" snaps Joss.

"Wrong. Infatuation can do stupid things to people." Hunter walks across and looks down at Portia on the ground, poking her with his Converse. "Aren't you going to stand and confront me, dearest queen? Scared?"

"Go to hell," she snarls.

"No, thanks. There's not a lot of room there anymore. Plus, the weather's nicer here. Better food sources too." He points at me and Joss. "But these assholes are really causing problems. All we want is our friends and family to join us, and they keep the portals closed. Really not cool, guys."

I drag a hand through my hair. This is wrong. Demons shouldn't be able to enter a fae home; Portia has warding and security, the place under constant surveillance.

And the demons shouldn't be able to stop us reaching them.

"How are they keeping us out?" snarls Joss as Ewan appears behind.

"He's warded the room." Ewan points upwards. An iridescent, circular rune painted on the ceiling glows.

There're few things that interfere with our powers and fewer still who know how to use what can.

More worrying, I've never seen this particular rune before.

Panic rises as I spin around to Ewan. "Where's Vee?"

"Downstairs with the kid."

"Don't fucking leave her! What if more of the bastards are around?"

Joss shakes his head. "There aren't. I can't sense any."

"And why the hell didn't you tell us there were demons in the house?"

"I couldn't sense them, okay?" he snaps back, but his face traces worry I share. He always senses demons nearby, but not this time.

Hunter claps his hands together. "Boys? Your attention please?"

What the fuck do I do? If Xander were here, he'd launch everything he had on pushing through whatever barrier exists between us. He'd have a chance at breaking through the runic magic, but none of us holds the same brute strength. Sure, if I could reach the barrier's other side I'd end the bastard, but how do we obliterate the rune?

The top door to the cellar remains open, and I toy with the idea of charging down there to grab Vee. If anything happens to her....

Hunter sighs and clicks his fingers. "Seriously? Can I have your attention here? In case you haven't noticed, I have the queen of the local fae lying on the floor and her daughter well... under duress."

The large demons remain focused on their victims, not engaging with events around them, automatons fulfilling a role. "Let them go," I snarl, "or you'll bloody regret it."

"Nope. You're the ones who will regret today."

"Sure," snorts Ewan.

Demon asshole rubs his hands together. "Some of the more sensible fae are coming over to our idea of a future for this world, but the problem is the majority believe you four are the good guys. I'm going to change that." He nods at the demon who stands over Portia, and the creature raises the chain. She whimpers and covers her face with her hands.

No. I charge at the barrier again, and the magic hits me like a high voltage electrical shock.

This is bullshit.

"So, we got to thinking, myself and some friends, how could we change the fae's opinion?" He points at himself. "*I* had the perfect solution." His face transforms into a smug grin, eyes flashing with excitement. "Imagine what would happen if one of their queens dies and the Four Horsemen are implicated."

“What the fuck?” I growl.

“Injured beyond the possibility they could heal her.” He raises his voice. “Viktor. Go ahead.”

Panic joins the anger as the hulking demon wraps the chain around his hands. I'm powerless to do anything as the iron whips Portia across the chest, tearing her jacket through to her skin. The scream sickens me.

"We won't be implicated because you won't kill her!" I shout.

"Yes, you will because there'll be no trace of us, only the queen's and daughter’s bodies. I'm sure her advisers are aware who was visiting the most important fae in the realm today."

Beside me, Ewan rubs his fingers together, concentrating on creating the invisible diseases or viruses he can conjure from the smallest microbes around him. Diseases that can kill instantaneously or infect and spread to others as quickly. But what's the point? We can't touch the bastard through his protection.

"This has never happened before," he mutters.

“Joss!” I look behind me. “Check on Vee and Kailey.”

The demon holds the chain in the air again. "Wait!" I yell. "Stop. Talk about this!"

Hunter gives the signal to his henchman to lower the chain. "Talk? Why?"

"Make a deal," I say through gritted teeth.

"Not interested. Which one first?" He points between the two women. "Or at the same time. I think it would be cruel for one to witness the other dying."

"Fuck!" I shout and step back, preparing to throw the full force of my power.

Death runs through me, I can kill with a touch if I'm in the right mind—like fucking furious—but I also have the ability to project an energy that stops hearts. In this form, demons have hearts I can wreck. Keeping this power under control takes a lot of effort, and my slip up the other night, killing the fae, brought us to this point today.

If I hadn’t killed the fae, we wouldn’t be summoned to explain ourselves. Without my actions, there’s no chance we’d be here at the time the demons planned.

They knew. The demons fucking knew that I'd reach the point I did to protect Verity; their stalking her and causing me to intervene guaranteed an uncontrolled reaction.

Somebody out there knows my weakness.

Magic surges through, death building in my hands, which crackle with an electrical power. The fury grips and the power surges, shooting from my fingertips in a lightning arc towards the demon's chest.

The energy hits the barrier, revealing the size as the lightning ball dissipates and crackles upwards and outwards along the previously invisible wall.

"Where's this magic from?" I shout. "How is the ward so strong against me?"

Hunter launches into a song and dance, chilling words about death and destruction likely from one of the emo bands he listens to with Elyssia. He gives the nod to the demon with the chain. The demon raises the chain again, and I fight covering my ears against the scream accompanying the thrash.

I stare ahead. Helplessness isn't an emotion I'm familiar with.

14

VERITY

Each time the woman's voice screams, Kailey shuffles closer to me and looks up with her large eyes filled with fear. I keep the light conversation going, but how can I calm her in this situation?

Urgent voices sound outside the basement window, above us, and I raise my voice in an attempt to prevent Kailey hearing. My chest tightens as my imagination runs wild. What if they break through the window? Someone comes down here? How can I protect us both with one knife? No, something happening publicly is a good thing because someone will alert the authorities.

I startle as the door flies open again, turning my body to shield the little girl. Kailey grips the back of my jacket and lets out another cry as a man steps into the room.

He's tall, solidly built—and brandishing a knife.

Anger rolls from him; face darkened and coiled to attack. Holy shit, there's no way I can defend myself against him. I stand, willing one of the other guys to run downstairs and help.

Then I notice the colour of his eyes, and the recognition crossing this guy's face. His hair's lighter and shorter than his brother's, but the full and sensual mouth matches. He tucks the knife back into his green combat jacket pocket, eyes flicking across my face, searching for confirmation.

"Verity." Not a question, but a gruff statement. His voice is low, the same English accent as the others.

Xander? Stupefied, I nod.

"Xander!" Joss steps into the room and shoves him in the chest. "Where the fuck have you been?"

Xander straightens and holds his face close to Joss's. "Does that matter right now? Get the hell up there and kill those bastards."

"We're trying. He's warded the fucking room!"

"I'm here now. Stop wasting time. Stay with her." He jabs a finger at Kailey. "Verity. Come with me."

This is one man who, in his current state, I don't want to argue with. When I hesitate, he grabs my hand and a painful jolt shoots up my arm. The other guys cause a tingling sensation when we touch, but the reaction to Xander bloody hurts.

Xander's brow furrows as I wince and cry out. He releases my hand. "What's wrong?"

"That."

"Good."

I balk. "What?"

"Can we not hang around for a Q&A session!" He

snaps his head round to Joss again. “I've taken out their friends guarding the house, but they're not kidding about killing her."

"Xander!" hisses Joss and inclines his head to the girl. Thankfully Kailey has her hands over her ears, but my heart wrenches as tears spill onto her cheeks.

"Kill?" I breathe.

"Yeah and frame us as responsible. That's one lie that's gonna cost us and threaten everything. Time to shine, sweetheart." Xander grabs my hand again and yanks me towards him. I stumble and steady myself on his chest, as more painful energy courses into me.

"What can I do?" I ask.

"Are you pussyfooting around her?" he snaps at Joss.

"Give us a chance. She’s only been with us twenty-four hours."

"For fuck's sake!" I shake as Xander grabs my other arm and holds me close; I’m overwhelmed by the anger filling my body, and my fear switches to a desire to run up the stairs and confront whoever’s there. Lying pisses me off and in the past has led to mild ranting at shocked recipients, but the desire to end whoever is up there grows with the realisation what’s happening. Frame the Horsemen? Telling the fae race they killed their queen? That’s one hell of a lie.

Something unknown flickers across Xander's face, and he switches to holding my cheeks in both hands. "Trust me. We can do this. Just channel what you feel from me."

Images assault my mind, the way they did with Heath yesterday, and I attempt to move, but Xander holds my cheeks harder. *A woman lying on the floor, a girl held against the wall, snapshots that flash by as if a camera moved past the room. This house. Mother and daughter. Demons.* I gasp and stare back at Xander whose eyes blaze with an intensity I share, aware his lips are close to mine, and freaking out over what happened when I was this close to Heath.

"Shit!" He drops his hold and backs up.

But I understand. Reaching out to him, I curl my fingers around his. "Go!"

Xander runs up the stairs, and I take two steps at a time behind as I follow. The uncomfortable charge inside my body grows, and as we burst into the room.

I barely have time to register the scene before a demon, twice the size of her, lashes Portia with a huge chain, adding to the welts already across her slim figure.

The anger explodes as the young guy in the room's centre laughs, and the energy held inside floods to the surface.

This. Ends. Now.

HEATH

A blinding light fills the room, and I cover my eyes, scared the intensity will fuck up my sight completely. Instantaneously, a thunderous noise fills the house, an assault on my other senses.

I hear glass splintering as pictures crash from the shaking walls, the floor moving beneath our feet, and I snap my eyes open as I steady myself on the doorframe.

Verity stands the other side of where the invisible

barrier existed, and Xander stands besides, gripping her hand.

Where the fuck did he come from?

I've heard Xander's magic explode before, sometimes destroying buildings or ripping through the air and tearing apart nearby enemies, but never accompanied by light too.

"You guys are so fucking dumb!" he shouts. At us or the demons? "Kill the bastards!"

This time the death shooting from my hands lands squarely in each demon's chest, and they sink to the ground with electrical tendrils covering their bodies. The chain drops from the first demon's hands as he writhes against the crackling electricity, and Ewan strides over to grab hold before the shocked guy can move.

The queen and her daughter crawl to the wall and cower as the room fills with noise and light again.

I don't need asking twice, as I stride over to the younger demon and slam a foot into his chest. He stares back at me, eyes widened by shock, but not fear. Yeah, I can kill instantly if I want, but some deserve something more painful than that.

"Ewan?"

"Gladly."

I can never see Ewan's created viruses cross the space between him and victims, but always the result. The demon who masqueraded as the guy who cared for Elyssia draws in a shaky breath and clutches his chest. His eyes widen and blood builds in his mouth, bubbling from between his lips as he struggles to speak. I withdraw my boot from his chest, and he crawls onto his hands and knees. A hacking cough erupts from his mouth and blood continues to spill from his mouth and spreads towards his hands on the spotless tile floor.

I stare down impassively. The bastard deserves this. I've no doubt he'd fulfill his mission and murder the two women in the room.

Xander and Vee still face away, hands connected; I wait for more exploding energy to come from the pair. Whatever surrounds them, the prone demons can't move as I stand over them.

"Go ahead," sneers one in a gravelly voice, eyes flashing red. "There's more where we came from."

I don't need asking twice. Lightning bolts from my hands as I hold both palms towards his chest. He jolts for an instant before his heart stops, and I turn to the second. The fear in his eyes doesn't faze me as I kill him. He'll never possess a scrap of humanity.

I need to get the girls out of here.

I help Portia to her feet, and she struggles to walk as Ewan guides her from the room. The red welts across her body, beneath her ripped clothes twist anger in my stomach. I've never seen a fae queen weakened like this, or believed anybody had a remote chance of reaching Portia. Where are her guards? What happened to the barrier against dark magic surrounding her home?

This shit is worse than we thought.

Elyssia wraps her arms around her knees, tears streaking dark eye make-up down her cheeks, as she stares at the dead body nearby.

"Are you okay?" I ask and crouch next to her.

Elyssia glares at the demon, face set hard. "They won't win. Never."

"No." Her bravery fills me with hope; the fact she won't yield even when her life's threatened in this way. But that's the fae. Proud. Fighters. Determined. They've survived in this world as long as they have because of their tenacity, and the demons know how strong they are too. "Come on."

In the corner of my eye, Verity sinks to the floor, and Xander catches her also crouching down to say something. She can't take her eyes from his, almost as if she's unaware of us around her. Xander breaks her gaze and blinks in my direction, the nod informing me exactly what I expected.

Xander experiences the same effect around her, and we witnessed the reason why.

"What happened?" I ask him.

"This is the whole bloody point she was created, Heath. The may've strengthened their forces against us, and I have no fucking idea how they found something this strong, but we have more now."

Verity looks up, eyes wide. "What the hell?"

"Your power fuelled mine." He looks to me in triumph. "This is gonna work!"

"Wow." I slump to the floor, and rest my head against the wall. "This is fucked up. Do you think the Order really intended to kill them?"

"Yeah. I've been tracking the bastards for two weeks."

"Why didn't you tell us? Jesus, man."

"And alert the Order I knew they were planning something? Ewan's ability to mess up their communications only goes so far." He gestures at the house. "They didn't just ward against us, they have the whole property glamoured. They couldn't manage this alone. They have fae help. We need to talk to Portia about what's really happening in her kingdom."

"She doesn't know," mumbles Elyssia. "Others on our council have been summoned here recently and sent to investigate. Nothing happens."

I run both hands down my cheeks. "And the portal threat you drove to, Xander? Are the deaths connected to vamps?"

"Red herring," mutters Xander. "Someone wanted us apart."

"I am so fucking confused. Who shifted the goal posts?"

"She did." Xander points a finger at Vee whose mouth parts in surprise. "I told you. Now she's with us, they need to step up their game, and so do we."

VERITY

I don't know whether to throw up or run screaming from the house; either way I'll never escape.

My debut as a human floodlight freaked the hell out of me, but Xander's hand in mine offered a reassurance I needed.

Exhausted and unharmed, I back away from the brothers and out of the room. I don't want to be around the scene in front of me.

Ewan tends to Portia in the kitchen where she rests against the kitchen island counter clutching her chest in one hand and a bottle of water in the other. Witnessing this in an ordinary suburban environment suddenly pushes bile into my throat. She might be fae, but here and now, she's a mother with two daughters in the house who's had her life threatened. Portia's struggle to remain impassive and pretend she's coping remains clear. Ewan looks over and nods at me.

Joss steps through the door leading to the basement, answering my question over where he's been. He holds Portia's daughter in his strong arms, Kailey's figure small against his large frame. The girl has hers wrapped around his neck, head on Joss's chest. He smiles his reassuring smile when he sees me, and warmth blooms inside at the care he's showing Kailey.

The little girl struggles from his arms and calls out when she sees her mum in the kitchen. Joss sets her gently on the floor.

"Good job on calming her down," I say. "She was screaming and terrified when Xander took me from the basement."

He chews on his lip. "I took her fear, Vee. I don't just starve people of positive emotions, but I take away negative too. You must've noticed me doing the same to you since you arrived at our house."

I blink at him. "What do you mean?"

"It strengthens me."

"By causing you to feel scared?"

He smiles wryly. "No. I don't feel the emotions, I just take them." My heart softens further as he looks to mum and daughter in the kitchen. "I hope she's okay."

I reach out and touch his cheek. "That was a beautiful thing to do."

"I did it because I could." He grips my fingers and a moment passes demonstrating what he described; my anxiety lowers, and I breathe slowly to help calm myself further. I want to stand here with him, stay calm, fuel the happiness I feel from being with him.

I want him to hold me and tell me none of this nightmare happened.

"Joss," says a voice.

He drops my hand as he looks over his shoulder at Heath. "Xander called for Portia's bodyguards, they're close by but oblivious to what happened."

"Shit." He elongates the word and my ebbing anxiety flows again.

"We need to go. I don't want to hang around to answer questions because her guys are pissed off. I don't think any encounter with them would end well."

"This is insane, Heath."

I don't miss them glance at me before looking back to each other. "Yeah, but when was life ever easy for us?"

15

VERITY

Living with four guys never appealed to me. I don't have siblings, and the male friends I knew at school were slobs. Living with four Horsemen? Also not on my ideal house-share-situation list.

While the guys "mopped up" at the queen's house (something I didn't want defining), I waited in the kitchen. Portia didn't stay, but took her daughters and headed upstairs without a word. So I sat on a stool, staring at my hands, freaking out that my skin still held an abnormal luminescence.

What the hell happened? How did I project light in that way? At first, I didn't realise the light emanated from me, closing my eyes against a brilliance that matched looking at the sun. Only when I looked down at Xander's hand in mine did I see the light surrounding me. Exactly what this ability to project light means scares me.

I'll add that to the list of “shit I can't deal with right now.”

Even as I sit here now, I can't comprehend recent events exist in reality.

Yeah, they do. Just a new and bizarre one.

How about this for added bizarre: the Four Horsemen sit around the kitchen table eating pizza and drinking beer as they discuss today's events and strategy. They don't exclude me, but I kept away from the conversation when the guys grilled Xander about his recent activities. I could ask them to give me a blow-by-blow account over what I am, or this is, the future, but for now, I'm too tired.

I sit at the head of the table, two guys either side of me, and enjoy a slice. Becoming a human floodlight sure takes it out of a girl.

"What happens next?" I ask them.

"We haven't decided," says Xander through a mouthful of pizza.

"But we're moving on, did you say?" I ask Heath.

"Not yet. We need to stay in the area until we've straightened out the events today." Xander's firm manner draws looks from Joss and Ewan and a scowl from Heath. "If we disappear from the area, we leave question marks over ourselves. The Order want rumours, and they want to reach us. We're bunkered down here and out of reach. Safe."

"But the magic the guy used today—that could breach our defences here," says Joss.

"The magic we beat?" Xander rests back in his chair

and takes a long drink from his beer. "We've got this. Especially now the Fifth is here."

"Verity," says Heath.

"Vee."

Joss and I speak my name at the same time, and he throws me one of his dimpled smiles.

I haven't had the chance to speak to Xander since he stepped away from me after the attackers died. He switched his sole focus to tidying up the aftermath left at Portia's house. I left with the other three guys; their relief was clear when Xander followed later and arrived home with the pizza and beer.

"So we're staying in Grangeton?" I ask. "Just so I know if I need to work tomorrow."

"Work?" Heath straightens. "Surely you're not going back to work."

"Why not? I can keep an eye on what's happening. Ewan said there're demons there. I can help."

Xander cocks a brow. "You're not scared to go?"

"No. Why should I be?"

"Because... demons?" he asks.

I stand. "I helped kill several today. I'm sure I can cope. Besides, Heath works there too."

"Ugh." Heath pulls a face. "I was only supposed to work there until we were sure you were the Fifth. I don't want to go back."

"She has a point," says Ewan. "Vee working at Alphanet will help me too; she can help hack into their computer system."

Xander raps the table with his long fingers. "No."

"Maybe this isn't your decision," I inform him.

Xander snaps his head around and narrows his eyes at me. "Excuse me?"

"I need to have some normality in my life."

"We do what's best for all of us. That's how we operate," he says in a low voice.

I hold his pissed off look. "Yes, and I've agreed to live with you and be part of this, but I'd like some control over my life."

"You can fool yourself you do, if you want," replies Xander. "But you don't have any control. None of us do. This is what we signed up for."

"I didn't sign up for anything!" I retort.

"Yes, you did," he snaps. "You just don't remember."

"Xander...," warns Ewan.

"How don't I remember? Until a few days ago I was just average me working my boring job!"

"And before then?" asks Xander.

"Before then I lived with a friend in the same flat, she left and—"

"Have you seen her since?" he asks.

"No, but."

"How about your family? Visited them recently?" Xander's focus on me is as unrelenting as his questions.

"Enough!" snaps Heath and stands. "Don't walk back in here and takeover, as if you have the right to do things the Xander way again."

"No, what does he mean, Heath?" I ask. "What happened to my family? Has someone hurt them?"

Joss stands abruptly and lifts his bottle. "Another beer anyone?"

I place my hand over Joss's, which silences him, and

the tension thickens in the room. "What happened to my family?"

"Nothing," mutters Xander and glances at Heath. "Nothing happened to them."

"Why the accusations, then?"

Xander waves a hand. "Fine. Go to work. Live your pretend life. I don't care as long as you come home and are here when we need you."

"Come home like a good girl?" I bark out a laugh. "Here when you need me? Hell, you sound like my new, abusive boyfriend."

Xander shoves his chair back and stands, his face dark. "No, Verity, I'm the one that holds this shit together."

"Oh yeah, when you're here," says Heath. "And don't talk to her like that!"

For the last day, I've managed to fight tears, but they well, and I fight them. Heath stands and approaches me, and I'm unaware my hands shake until he takes one. "Ignore him." He shifts to touch my cheek.

Xander's eyes widen and his mouth parts. "Ah! Right. I understand now." He stands too and approaches us. Heath steps between me and Xander, but I push him to one side. I don't need defending.

"What's happened between the two of you?" demands Xander.

"Nothing," he mutters.

I bristle. How do they put up with this guy's attitude? "He kissed me. I kissed him."

"What the fuck?" he hisses at Heath.

"Yeah, what the fuck?" asks Ewan. "Joss. Did you know?"

Joss blows air into his cheeks. "Yeah."

"Oh, this is fucking brilliant!" Xander throws his arms in the air. "Heath Landon's dick takes over, once again."

"I said we kissed!" I snap. "Nothing more happened and won't."

"Hah! She doesn't know your reputation then, Heath?" laughs out Xander.

"Like you're a saint around girls!"

"She's not just a girl though, is she?" Xander leans forward so he's in Heath's face, and I extend both arms to push them apart.

"I'm not a bloody toy to fight about! I'll kiss who I want!" I cringe at my teenage-style words. "I'm a girl who'll do whatever she wants, with whoever."

"You're not even a girl!" hisses Xander, cheeks flushing with anger.

"Correct! I'm a twenty-one year old woman."

"Bullshit. You don't even fucking exist!" he snaps.

Before I can catch up to his words or reply, Xander turns on his heel, grabs a bottle from the table, and marches out of the room. Still trembling, I look between the other guys in the room.

"Well, he's one big bundle of fun, isn't he?" I attempt a light tone, but his words echo. I don't exist?

Nobody responds; my humour falls flat. For the first time since my failed attempt to run from the whole situation, I want to leave. Singed bedroom carpet? If I can cope with demons, I can cope with minor decorative disasters at home.

The stupid tears build, and I turn my face away from Heath, scared he'll touch me and trigger a breakdown. Mistake, because my blurring eyes immediately meet Joss's.

No.

I'm stronger than this.

I won't let any of them see my weakness.

"Be right back!" My light tone is drowned out by a croaking voice. Great.

The kitchen's empty, thankfully Xander didn't head in here. I pour a glass of water and pause by the sink. What an asshole. I gulp the water.

"I told you my brother was a bit of an asshole," says Heath from behind, echoing my thoughts. "Are you okay?" He closes the kitchen door.

"This is all bloody confusing," I admit. "I'm not sure I can cope with much more."

The guy standing in the kitchen with me looks like the extraordinarily attractive, but ordinary guy I thought invited me on a date. I focus on reimagining him as the guy from work who paid me attention, all muscle-bound six feet plus of gorgeousness, and not a man who has the power to kill in seconds.

Inside, a part believes he is; that if I'd never discovered who Heath is, or what I am, we could've developed into more.

Heath nods. "I'm sorry I never spoke to you about the kiss, but I didn't want you to think it meant anything."

My chest tightens, but what right do I have to be hurt by his words? I'm attracted to the other guys as much as to him, which confuses the hell out of me.

But I met him in my world before being dragged into this one. Heath's the guy from work who I sparked with, despite the pouring rain and fact I ran him down in my car.

Stupid, Verity...

"Okay." I turn away back to the sink, remembering Ewan's words about choosing all of them, or none.

"Xander's angry I screwed up. He'll calm down."

"Can we not talk about this?" I turn. "Maybe explain to me what he means about how I don't exist."

"No, Vee. Xander was just being a dick."

I narrow my eyes at him. "You're from my real world, Heath. You know the real Verity."

"Not really."

I move towards him, desperate to touch and convince myself I'm real, that the energy that charged between us when we first kissed and touched was a normal, everyday attraction. "Am I real?" I whisper.

"Yes." He touches my face. "So fucking real to me. To all of us."

"And how I feel about you. Is that real?" I grip his fingers.

"You look at Joss the same way as you do me, even Ewan, and I'm sure before Xander pissed you off you felt an attraction."

"No. Yes. Shit." I pull his hand away. "But you're all different men.

"And you're a part of us."

"I know. I'm here with you all."

Heath shakes his head and takes my face in his hands. "We're all part of each other. Inside. There's an energy that connects us, split five ways. More than connects, it bonds us and keeps us close to each other."

"The real reason I don't want to leave, huh?" I ask.

"And why whatever you feel is purely a physical desire too." His gaze drops to my mouth. "What I feel too. We all do."

"But you're different men; you don't have the same personalities. Whatever you are, there's a human side that I'm attracted to. This is more than..." I trail off.

Ewan already told me the reality.

I've witnessed how their personalities grip the guys and cause conflict between them. Add in sexual attraction for me, rather than the testosterone causing the guys to clash, and I'm at the centre of a perfect storm.

"This isn't just physical," I say. "Can't be."

Heath moves closer, body almost against mine as my back presses against the sink. "Maybe not, but this can't be anything else either."

I swallow. "This is bloody intense for two people who met less than a week ago."

"I think it's more than a week since you were checking out my ass, Vee," he says in a soft voice. He trails a finger across my lips and heat builds in my belly.

The buzz from his touch spreads across my face. "True. But you all have nice asses, so I suppose you can see my dilemma."

Heath smiles, but his eyes don't. "Exactly, it would be impossible to decide which piece of ass to choose."

"Ah well, maybe I'll just have all four." I laugh and stop myself when his brow furrows. "Joking!"

Heath swears under his breath and rests his forehead against mine, warm breath mingling, his scent wrapping around and reminding me how soft his lips were against mine; how his taste intoxicated me. "Maybe one of us will persuade you otherwise."

"Don't," I whisper back. "Not again."

He cradles my head in his hands, and kisses my forehead, gentle and soothing. "But you're here, with me, and I'll fight to keep you safe. I'm going to really bloody struggle with keeping away from you because the human you recognises the human me. This isn't just some bullshit supernatural connection."

My throat thickens. Why couldn't an ordinary guy be the one saying these words to me? His warm skin against mine, the familiar charge between us, takes control of the situation and I move my face to place my lips on his. The moment I push my mouth on his, Heath claims my mouth in a sudden, intense kiss. His hands move so he's holding my face, and I press myself against him. Heath grabs my waist and pulls me flush against his chest as he deepens the kiss. My senses fill with his scent and taste, but also the coursing power between us.

I forget myself and tangle my body and tongue with his, everything and everybody around fading to nothing. I grasp at keeping the world upright, scared Heath will pull me away from the tiny grip I still have.

I circle his neck with my hands and dig fingers into his hair, gripping onto him the way he is me, in a kiss unlikely to stop any time soon. He grabs my ass, pushing me harder against the sink.

I tear my mouth away, desperate to bring some oxygen into the situation, and Heath switches to gentle kisses along my neck and collarbone. His heated breath comes in short bursts as he slides both hands beneath my shirt and along my sides. His hands are as warm as the soft lips, heating as his desire grows.

The harder I push against him, the more aware of his arousal I am, and the barrier between us does nothing to stop the wet heat building between my legs.

I slip my hands beneath his shirt too, resisting the

urge to unbutton, and place hands on the impressive abs I knew were there. The thought tightens everywhere, and I drag my fingers along the ridges. His grip on my waist intensifies, fingers digging hard into my skin.

A noise nearby jerks me back to awareness, and I push at Heath, rubbing my lips together, eyes locked on his. Every nerve in my body's lit up, and if he touches me again, I swear I will combust.

Heath steps back and squeezes his eyes closed. "Hell, Vee."

We stand, hands on each other's faces and share the unspoken understanding that this needs to stop before the situation runs out of control. Today demonstrated a need for unity amongst the Four. There're enough issues with the demons' attempts to conquer the guys, without the Fifth who's supposed to help instead causing a bigger rift.

"I think I need some time alone," I whisper.

"We can figure this out."

"I have a lot to deal with right now, Heath." I drop my hand and dip my head, not wanting to see if his emotions reflect mine.

Only when he moves back does oxygen rush back into my lungs and clear my dizzy head. Then suddenly he crushes me in his arms, against his chest and holds the back of my head. I inhale his scent, fighting the tears as his warm breath heats my scalp. I could stand here all night, allow him to hold me in place as the seismic shift happens beneath my feet.

But I can't.

This can't happen.

I move my hands between us and push gently at his chest. "Heath."

Heath releases me and moves away, chewing on his bottom lip as he does. "I meant what I said. I will always be here for you. Always."

I can't... I stumble through the door and along the narrow hallway, almost slipping on the slate tiles in my stockinged feet. I grab the stair rail and pull myself up two at a time, desperate for my one last sanctuary, my borrowed bedroom. As I open the door, the tears finally spill down my cheeks and I drag in a shuddering breath.

Ewan appears besides me and grabs my arm. "Vee? Are you okay? I saw you run through the house."

Shit. I wipe my face with a jacket sleeve and then turn to him. "I'm okay."

"No. It was wrong of him to say that to you."

What? "I'm okay," I repeat.

"Seriously, I'm fucking furious, and he's obviously finished the story and upset you more." I widen my eyes in confusion. "Xander. What he's told you, it's not a hundred percent true."

"Isn't it?"

Ewan frowns. "It's not easy to handle when you're told you never existed until three years ago. He should've been gentler."

The hallway lurches, floor sliding beneath my feet. "You?"

"What?"

"What do you mean that you never existed? Or do you mean me?"

He studies me with his intense green eyes. "Shit."

I grasp his arm, to hold myself upright as much as

anything else. "Are you telling me I'm not real? What are you telling me?" My voice rises, hysteria edging in. "Ewan!"

"Fuck," he growls. "Fuck."

"Tell me!" I shout and grasp his shirt tighter. "Don't do this to me!"

Footsteps thump up the stairs, and I spin around to see Joss. "What the hell are you doing, Ewan?"

I dig fingers into my hair and tug hard, confirming the pain is as real here as inside my tightening chest. "He says I'm not real!"

"No. I didn't say that," says Ewan. "Vee, calm down."

I straighten and fight the desire to lash out—or run—and look Ewan straight in the face.

"Tell me. Am I Verity Jameson? Did I grow up in Grangeton with my parents? Have I worked at Alphanet for five years?"

He doesn't answer.

The silence throws a tsunami over my body, knocking me backwards. I slump against the wall and slide to the floor, keeping my eyes fixed on Ewan's as Joss remains frozen next to me. Neither man's eyes hold the answer I want.

"Who am I?"

16

EWAN

How the fuck do I deal with this situation? Vee's trying her hardest not to, but she's crying. Her pale shock means she can't control everything happening inside her mind right now, or with her body.

I made her cry.

The thought sickens me.

Vee's torn apart, and it's my dumb fault for presuming the worst.

Xander's an asshole, especially when he's back from time away, immersed in stress. How was I to know Xander never found Vee and revealed the whole truth? Hell, I've been the one insisting we do, but I held this information back.

I don't answer her question, fully aware Vee would

know I lied and that the truth would destroy her fragile grip on what's left of her reality.

Is this a mistake?

She shifts from staring us in the face, eyes welling with tears to staring at her hands. Vee mumbles to herself, and a cold fear grips my chest that the logical, sensible girl I spoke to, when we spent alone time the other night, has been pushed too far.

"Vee?"

She turns cold eyes to mine. "You lied."

"I haven't. I didn't reply."

Her lips thin. "Exactly."

What the fuck do I do here? Girls? Don't bother with them beyond hook-ups. Our lifestyle on the road, living one place for weeks at the most, doesn't lead to meaningful relationships, and we spend time with girls who understand the score.

But Vee.

Holy fucking fuck *Vee.*

Xander announced she existed, informed us what the deal would be between us and her. I shrugged his ridiculous ideas away. No way would a member of the opposite sex affect me in a way I can't control. Normally, I shut down, don't deal, keep away.

Then her. The girl Heath refused to talk too much about when he started working at Alphanet. All he told us is she's Verity and he was aware of the pull to her. Why didn't he elaborate?

The night I met the achingly beautiful Verity in the pub, I pulled on the gruff Ewan and practically held my breath against her effect. Her attraction to Heath was, and still is, plainly obvious. I'll continue to hide mine to her.

Our one touch remains etched in my mind; my fingers against her hair and skin, the evening we spent alone together. During those hours, our common interests added to the Horsemen connection. We share a passion for seeking the truth.

And now this.

Verity's cheek rests on her knees, drawn into her chest, head turned away from us. I hold my hands out to Joss in a “what do we do?” gesture. He shakes his head and the silent stand-off begins.

Who tells her? Who will be the one Verity hates for breaking the news?

I rehearse the words in case I'm the one who needs to speak them.

You are human, but not the one you thought you were.

Don't worry; you do exist. You've existed for years. Just not your whole life.

Fuck. No. I can't explain this.

"Joss?" I whisper.

"I don't fucking know what to say."

My story planning begins again, ready for more questions from Vee. There's no way to break this gently, or rationally.

Verity. Your life is a lie. The past you hold memories of doesn't exist. Why don't you ever see your parents? Where are your friends? I push down much I need to say. *They don't exist. None of what you believe is true.*

Paralysis in a situation isn't a useful state, or common for us. I care for Vee, heart aching for her. Joss doesn't look as if he's fairing much better. Is his ability strong enough to calm Vee and allow her to listen rationally to the greatest headfuck of her time?

"I don't think sitting on the hallway floor is the best place for this conversation," Joss says in gentle tones. He crouches beside Vee and attempts to take her hand.

Vee snatches her fingers away and wraps her arms around her head again, her chest rising and falling rapidly, her breath coming in short bursts.

"Is she having a panic attack?" I whisper to Joss.

"Are you surprised? You dumb fucker!"

"I was trying to help explain the situation. I thought Xander had told her." He screws his face up at me. "Sorry, okay?"

Joss touches Verity on the back. "Come on, don't sit there."

The anguish on her face when she looks up at

him kills me; rips into my heart as if a demon's clawing it from behind my ribs.

I caused this.

I hurt her.

She attempts to shrug Joss's hand away, and I will him to succeed in using his powers on her.

"Vee...," he whispers.

"Get off me!" she screams at him. "Leave me alone!"

Joss's eyes widen for a second before he catches her flailing arms. I watch, broken heart in my mouth, as she lashes at him and he attempts to catch her arms. Her protests that we're lying, this isn't true rings in my ears until they're muffled by Joss holding her to him, sitting next to Vee and gripping her tight.

Seconds pass that feel like minutes as her breathing slows, face buried into Joss's chest as her fight against him wanes. He places a cheek on her hair and strokes her back as she lies in his arms.

I'm useless to Verity. Fucking useless, virus-spreading Pestilence. Joss can do this to help her; Heath already caught her attention and could probably help too. Xander? Well, I guess I'm further up the friendship scale than him.

Or I was.

I dig hands into my pockets. After today's events, I'm exhausted, the beers in my system tiring me more. I have an inkling how Vee feels, but on a tiny level. Demons breeching fae barriers and threatening lives, us risking accusations. Things have shifted for the Four too.

"Maybe you should go," says Joss. "I'll help Vee."

I clench my teeth. "Right. Should we tell Heath and Xander?"

Joss gives a vigorous shake of his head. "No. Heath will lose his shit and Xander's volatile right now. Leave this until the morning."

I watch Joss help Vee to her feet, her face calmer but no less stunned. "Come on, I think you need to lie down," he says to her.

"I uh... I'll bring her some water or something?" I wipe my face with both hands. "Something stronger?"

But my words aren't heard as Joss guides Vee into his bedroom.

I turn my back. Yeah, fucking useless me.

JOSS

Was this Ewan's need to tell Vee everything? Or a genuine mistake? Surely he couldn't be cruel enough to drop this on her, especially after today. If Vee finds her way through this and comes out the other side with acceptance, she's stronger than I thought.

Will the power inside that holds her to us manage to override her human reaction? Will the truth trump her disbelief and pain?

For now, all I'm aware of us the anguish emanating from her as Vee's warm figure lies in my arms. I've craved being this close to her since the first time I saw her, struggling not to, over and over, in situations I felt her need for calm. My reason why I avoided this? Because holding her arouses a need to not let her go, to kiss her the way I saw her with Heath even though every ounce of me knows this is wrong.

I sit on the edge of the bed, not letting go. Her wet cheeks are soft against my neck, and my arms surround her slim body. The lemon scent from her shampoo reminds me of cheesecake, and I laugh at the weird connection in my mind.

Vee, good enough to eat.

I grip her tighter and dismiss the thoughts distracting me from my efforts to impart calm in this frightened girl.

My back aches from holding her in the weird position, and I lie besides her, drawing her close. Vee doesn't respond; her face's still buried into my shirt, now damp with her tears.

Why did those who created the Five Horsemen do

this to her? The news Verity existed, confused us. Why wasn't she with us? They'd hidden Truth in the world and wiped her memories, replacing them with false ones. How's that for bloody ironic. Why? I have no fucking idea, but one day I'm going to find out and give them Hell.

I suspect this was to keep her secret from those who'd only heard of the Four Horsemen and focused their energies on working against our combined powers. Xander's convinced she holds something more important, besides amplifying those powers. A link to the portals?

Xander's correct—we signed up for this, but I don't remember when or why either. I'm just Joss. Famine. No history or memories. Nothing. All I remember is instinctively knowing the task at hand, protect the world. Occasionally flashes I think are memories cross my mind: darkness, fear, carnage. I dismiss them every time. Perhaps I don't want to remember where I came from.

At least I didn't go through what Verity is right now.

"Vee?" I ask, tentative, tensing against her freaking out again.

For the first time, her arms encircle my neck as she pushes herself closer. I tense again, this time at her lips on my neck as she speaks.

"You're doing it again, aren't you?" she says.

I shift at the effect her soft mouth on my skin has. Really, Joss, totally inappropriate.

"Calming you? Yes. This time I had to be closer to you."

"I don't want to believe this," she whispers. "I feel like I'm going to throw up."

"What, now?" I ready myself to move, and her breath tickles my skin as she laughs softly.

"No. Now I just want to close my eyes and forget. Maybe when I wake up one of you will tell me it's not true."

"Nobody can lie to you, Vee," I bury my face in her hair and inhale.

"I know." Vee's breathing speeds again, and I hold her closer, focusing every ounce of energy I have on soothing the new pain washing from her to me.

"Do you want me to leave you to sleep?" I ask.

Her arms tighten. "No. I think I need the special Joss treatment. Unless you have a shed-load of Valium."

I laugh, but my chest hurts, exhaustion passing through me too.

"I'll stay," I say. "I want you to rest."

Vee doesn't move as I pull the blankets from the bed over us.

I doubt I'll sleep anytime soon.

OTHER BOOKS BY LJ SWALLOW

The Four Horsemen Series

Reverse Harem Series

Legacy

Bound

Hunted

Other titles coming late 2017

The Soul Ties series

New Adult Paranormal Romance/Urban Fantasy

Fated Souls: A Prequel Novella

Soul Ties

Torn Souls

Shattered Souls

Touched By The Dark

Paranormal romance/Urban fantasy

ACKNOWLEDGMENTS

A special thanks to a few people who have helped me find my way in this new project. I've been welcomed into the reverse harem community by such a wonderful group of people. Thanks especially to Ashley Leanne Pelham, Soobee Dewson and Samantha Bruner for beta reading the book.

Thanks also to all the lovely readers who joined the Four Horsemen readers group and shared my excitement for the series.

Thank you to Krys Janae from TakeCover Designs for designing such a beautiful cover at short notice and for her patience!

And again, thanks to Peggy for her editing excellence and friendship.

ABOUT THE AUTHOR

LJ Swallow is a USA Today bestselling paranormal romance and urban fantasy author who is the alter-ego of bestselling contemporary romance author Lisa Swallow.

Giving in to her dark side, LJ spends time creating worlds filled with supernatural creatures who don't fit the norm, and heroines who are more likely to kick ass than sit on theirs.

For more information:

ljswallow.com
lisa@lisaswallow.net